Prudence felt the color rise in her neck. "We're not talking about me, sir. We're discussing the child."

"You may be talking about the child, sweet creature of heaven. I am talking about you. Are you honest? I don't know who I am and I freely admit it. Do you know who you are?"

"I am Prudence Drake," she said, and hated to hear the frantic, unsure tones in her own voice.

"And who is that? A governess, very prim, very proper. Have you ever let your hair down?"

"What do you mean? Of course!"

"No, I don't mean when you comb it out at night and instantly trap it back into a severe plait again. I mean: have you ever let your hair down and run along a beach in your shift, or pulled out your pins because a warm breeze is blowing from the summer sky and you want to feel long tendrils caress your bare arms. Have you ever let down your hair in front of a man?"

A flood of uncomfortable heat coursed through her body. "Oh, good gracious! This is absurd and outrageous, sir!"

FOLLY'S REWARD

Jean R. Ewing

Zebra Books
Kensington Publishing Corp.
http://www.zebrabooks.com

*"If thou remember'st not the slightest folly
That ever love did make thee run into,
Thou hast not loved."*

—As You Like It

Prologue

"By God, travel is tiresome. Where the devil are we?"

The young man's voice seemed slurred with drink. He had been lounging gracefully on the coach seat as if asleep, but now he lifted thick, dark lashes and glanced from the window.

"Never mind where we are, Grey, you're too foxed to remember even if I told you."

"Not too foxed for vice, sir." Rich black hair fell over the man's forehead above a face boned finely enough to be unforgettable.

"Do you have adventurous tastes, Mr. Grey?" It was a drawl, filled with unpleasant insinuation.

"Try me," said the young man with a slow smile. He leaned his dark head against the cushions of the carriage and listened to the harsh crunch of snow under the wheels, before closing his lids over eyes of a remarkably deep blue. "We are barely into the second week of the new year, sir. 1814 was deuced dull in my opinion. I am game for anything new that 1815 can show me—especially if she is clean of pox, sir, and speaks English."

"Like a nice game pullet?" The speaker gave the other three gentlemen a broad wink, and nodded knowingly at the young man who had joined their company by proving himself a wilder drinker and deeper pocket than any of them.

One of the other men spoke in an unpleasant whisper. "You never saw such a den of vice, sir! Madame Relet's little *maison* has a certain reputation. I hope we're all game!"

The deep blue eyes remained closed as the young man slid serenely to the floor of the carriage.

"What the devil!" It was the man who had asked Mr. Grey about his tastes. The young man's elbow had caught him hard in the shin, forcing him to pull his legs aside.

The man of the unpleasant whisper fared worse. A booted foot momentarily crushed his hand against the seat, causing him to curse and threaten retribution.

"Forget it," said the man next to him, jerking his own feet out of the way. "He's foxed. Mr. Grey has no idea where we are or what's intended tonight. He can't even see straight."

"Oh, can't I?" asked the supposed Mr. Grey.

He lay back among the booted feet of his companions, forcing them to make room for him or risk further injury. In the next moment he had pulled out a small engraved pocket pistol. Everyone dived for cover as he began to shoot out the upholstered buttons inside the carriage top with deadly accuracy.

"We are almost to Paris," he said. "And even three sheets to the wind I can shoot straight."

Then he suppressed a most inappropriate upwelling of laughter. His name was not Grey.

Chapter 1

It was a glass-clear morning, shining suddenly in the gray days of March as a golden coin glints among pebbles. Prudence opened her parasol and watched Bobby run erratically down the beach. She tried to let the brightness of the sea and sky calm her fears. They were safe here, surely?

The child stopped and examined something at his feet. His blond head was supported on such a fragile neck above his lace collar. The little trousers buttoned to his pleated muslin jacket were much the same color as his hair under the straw top hat, so that his entire figure seemed to blend into the pale wash of sand. The hat wobbled as he bent to pick up a shell. Prudence felt a rush of love and protection for him. It's very absurd, she thought, for a five-year-old child to have to carry such a thing on his head; I shouldn't make him wear it.

As if he heard the thought, Bobby took off the offending headgear and began to fill it with shells. He hunted through the sand, slowly moving away, until he disappeared for a moment behind the end of a long ridge of black rock, one of several that ran from the cliffs toward the sea. Prudence stood up and called to him. The child reappeared immediately with the hat clutched to his chest.

"Pray, do not go out of my sight, young man!" Her smile was tinged with anxiety. "It isn't the done thing, you know. I would not like it at all if I were to lose you." She walked up to him and bent down, though the front of her brown worsted skirt trailed in the sand. "Did you find many shells?"

Bobby looked up at her. "I cannot carry them all," he said seriously. "It's a hard thing to find so many wondrous things on the beach and to have to leave so many behind."

"But you would seem to have a veritable feast of shells in your hat." Prudence tried to hide her delight. Bobby would always enchant her. "Didn't you bring the very best ones?"

Bobby set down his hat and reached for her hand. "I found something much better than shells, Miss Drake. I think you would like it, too. I found a man."

"Did you? Was he a shell man or a seaweed man?"

"No! No!" Bobby's shrill voice was filled with honest indignation. "A real man! He looks like the man from the song about the seals and he talks a magic language. He's here, behind the rock. Don't you want to see?"

"Very well," she said, humoring the child. "But then we must go."

The proffered hand was slightly sticky with salt. Following Bobby's sturdy little straw-colored figure, Prudence stepped to the other side of the rock shelf.

"Oh, good gracious," she said, dropping both the child's hand and her parasol. "It is a real man!"

The man was young, with an air of strength about him even though he lay abandoned and unconscious against the rock. His serge trousers and unbuttoned reefer jacket were soaked and discolored with saltwater. He wore no cravat, and his shirt was torn at the front revealing the curve of taut muscle across his rib cage. One hand, partly lying in a shallow tide pool, lay turned up on the sand. It was well-formed and strong, with marked blisters across the palm. Yet it seemed he took care of his nails, and his sodden boots were of very fine quality. Prudence moved a little closer and leant down to look at his face. Beneath a thatch of midnight hair, slick with salt water, the lines of his nose and chin were clean and hard, beautifully structured. Long black lashes lay against the high cheekbones, yet they were not curved like her own, but thick and straight. As she hesitated, the lashes lifted a little. Prudence had the impression for a moment that his eyes reflected the sky, before they closed again.

"Oh, gracious!" she said, jumping back. "He's alive!"

"Of course he's alive," replied Bobby. "He already looked at me before."

The eyes remained closed, but his lips moved a little. Prudence found herself watching them with an immodest fascination. Very attractive lips.

"*Diable!*" muttered the man. "*Nous ferons naufrage! Vogue la galère!*"

"It is a magic language, isn't it?"

"No, I'm sorry." Prudence could feel her heart leaping and pounding in her breast. "It isn't the silkie's language, Bobby. This man is French."

The man turned his head toward her and revealing eyes the color of harebells looked straight up into hers. He smiled. "Not French, ma'am. I am sure of that at least."

It was a perfectly modulated and very cultured English, with no trace of the soft Scots accent that colored her own. An Englishman, then.

"But see!" said Bobby. "His eyes are blue, like the silkie's."

To her immense surprise, the man laughed. He blinked against the bright sun for a moment, then pulled his hand out of the shallow pool to shade his eyes. He grimaced as moisture ran from his fingers onto his face. "By God, they are eyes filled unaccountably with salt. No doubt the blue is shot through with red, like the Union Flag. I feel as if I just took the worst from the knuckles of Gentleman Jackson." Very carefully he felt the back of his skull and winced. "And a crack to the pate, alas. No wonder I am witless."

"What are you doing here?" Prudence had the wildest desire to run away and leave this unsettling find to wash away with the next tide.

He looked at her and grinned. His teeth were very white and even. "As to that, I have no idea. Is there some human habitation hereabouts, or are you an angel sent to accompany this charming cherub—in which case I shall never have cause to care for comfort again? I hate to admit it, but at this moment I am devilish cold. I believe I may have been in the ocean all night."

"Oh, good heavens! You must think me entirely lacking in wits! Are you shipwrecked? From the storm last night?"

The man slowly sat up and ran one hand over his hair, brushing it back from his forehead. The fingers shook a little. "I suppose I must be."

"What do you mean, you must be? Do you not know?"

He looked about him, at the sun-washed beach and the scattering of sea birds. "I am most dreadfully afraid that I do not."

"But where do you come from? What is your name?"

He reached a little unsteadily for the rocks to pull himself to his feet. Prudence reached out a hand and he took it. It was obvious that he was considerably taller than she, even though he partly supported himself against the rocks. He smiled down at her, and did not let go of her fingers. "It would seem, dear angel, that I am a foolish idiot, for however ramshackle it might appear to you, I don't know that either."

Prudence was uncomfortably aware that the grip of his naked hand against hers was most improper, though it was not at all unpleasant. She tried to ignore it. "You don't know who you are?"

"I can do nothing but supply you with doggerel. Rhymes ran through my head all night, though heaven only knows why." He laughed. "Things like this:

A sodden young fellow was found
as he lay without name on the ground
though spared by the waves
his fate was a knave's
to be hanged for a rogue when not drowned.''

He turned her fingers over in his. ''What a shoddy bit of verse!
My apologies.''

''But you must know your own name!'' Prudence persisted.

''Like Abou Hassan, I might believe I am the caliph, for
I'm damned if I know otherwise. I think my name might begin
with 'P'—no, 'H', perhaps. Or perhaps I have the name that
Achilles took when he hid among women? A deuced depressing
thought, since no one knows it.''

Prudence tried to pull her hand away. ''Sir, I beg you will
remain here while I go for help.''

He was running his fingers over hers, as if counting them.
''I would much rather you stayed here with me, angel.''

''My name is Miss Prudence Drake, sir.''

''Miss? Then in spite of the golden hair you share, this
cherub isn't yours? For I can tell without asking that you are
a lady of unimpeachable virtue.''

Prudence blushed scarlet. ''I am a governess, sir. Bobby is
in my charge.'' Then she realized that she had told him the
truth as if it didn't matter. She could easily have given a false
name, pretended that Bobby was her child; no one would be
looking for a mother and her son.

''You are ill, sir,'' she snapped. ''Pray, let me get help from
the house.''

''Then there is a house. A nice, square, ordinary house, I
hope, with a fire and a kettle simmering over the hob? You
won't take me back to your fairy castle and put me under some
spell, will you? I should hate to live out my days as a merry
little pig among enchanted swine.''

Bobby giggled and Prudence shook her head, surprised into laughter which she bit back. "It's just a small manse, sir."

The man grinned. "Excellent. No doubt in a minute or two I shall be perfectly competent to propel myself there with only a modicum of help from you."

"And from me, sir?" asked Bobby.

"Without question, young fellow."

"Until then, perhaps you might release my hand?" asked Prudence.

"Oh, no, I would much rather keep it. What remarkably long fingers you have, Miss Drake. I think I must gallantly kiss them as a mark of my gratitude for your rescue."

Prudence stood nervously in front of him as he carried her hand to his lips and kissed the back of her knuckles. It was done with a practiced grace. "You may not know your name, sir," she said. "And you are no doubt a victim of last night's wreck. But I don't think you are an ordinary sailor. In fact, I believe you may be some kind of villain!"

The blue eyes laughed into hers. "Do you? Good heavens, I don't think I'm a villain, truly. I shall try to prove myself merely a harmless, though possibly idiotic, gentleman, so that you may relax and feel moved to complete my rescue. In the meantime, do you mean to tell me that a ship foundered off this coast last night?"

"If you will return my hand to my own possession, sir, I shall tell you." With a rueful smile he dropped her fingers. Prudence stepped back, out of his reach. "There was a most dreadful storm last night and a brig from France was lost; it is thought she went down with all hands."

He looked thoughtfully at her. "From France?"

"So I was told. And since you did greet me with mutterings in French, I think we might assume that you have just come from that country."

"What did I say?"

"Well, you began with an oath." Prudence frowned at him

as sternly as she was able. "Then you mumbled something about a shipwreck and let come what may."

He stood and gazed out over the calm ocean for a moment. "If I was on that sad vessel, I would seem to have washed up to shore like Venus on her shell. Yet it all seems very deserted. Where is this interesting place?"

"This is Argyleshire. Unless you speak Gaelic, you would not be able to pronounce the name of the place."

"Good Lord! I'm in Scotland?" Suddenly he shivered. "Miss Drake, in spite of the clear sky, the beneficent sun, and the sweet, burning light of your own presence, it isn't warm on this beach."

"Oh, good gracious! Here, take my shawl!" Prudence held out her paisley shawl.

The man managed to peel off his soaking jacket and began to reach for the shawl. Then he dropped his hand and rubbed at his face. He was shaking a little. "Devil take it!"

"Pray remember your language, sir," said Prudence, with a glance at Bobby who was watching the man wide-eyed.

"I'm sorry, guardian angel, truly. But I seem to be as weak as a dandy after six bottles. May I prevail upon you to help me? I should indeed be grateful for the shawl, for I am regrettably ill-clothed, and it's most inappropriate to be wet when it's so deuced cold."

Prudence stepped up to him to drape her shawl around his shoulders. Instantly he caught her to him and pressed her body into his. She could feel the chill moisture from his shirt seeping into her dress. "You're very warm," he said with a shaky laugh against her ear. "Will you share a little?"

"Pray, sir, you don't help your cause! Do you want my assistance or not? For I am rapidly beginning to think I must leave you here to your fate."

"Then perhaps you should, for now I am disgracefully aware of a desire to kiss you, guardian angel." She could feel his lips moving against her hair. "If I am to die out here on this cold beach, that would be my password into Paradise. But instead I promise to be the soul of rectitude, dear Miss Drake, as sober and prudent as a dried apple, if you will but help me off this accursed beach. In the meantime, your shawl will transform me into a copy of your aged grandam, as harmless an old lady as ever walked this earth.''

He released her and stepped back. With a flourish, he managed to swing her shawl around his shoulders, and taking up her parasol, he opened it. In the next instant, he transformed himself into a caricature of a wizened old dame. In spite of herself, Prudence laughed. He was just a young man, full of nonsense and bravado, maybe no older than she was, and cold, and in shock. He needed help, not judgment.

"The house is not far," she said. "If you feel able to walk, follow me."

Prudence turned and took Bobby by the hand. The child pulled back and looked over his shoulder. The man was following, if a little unsteadily, his sodden jacket slung over his shoulder. Yet at the turn around the end of the rocks, he sat suddenly on the rock ledge and dropped his head to his knees. Prudence hurried back to him. He looked up and grinned.

"Don't discompose yourself, dear angel. Even Jonah was able to save himself, and he was swallowed whole and then regurgitated before being washed up."

"Oh, don't be silly," said Prudence. "Let me help you. Put your arm about my shoulders."

He shook his head, but Prudence put her hand around his waist and helped him stand. Beneath the wet shirt he was supple and lean, yet his flesh was icy cold under her fingers. Leaning against her, he walked up the beach, Bobby clinging to his other hand. Yet when they reached the straw hat full of shells, he bent to retrieve it and handed it to the little boy.

"I imagine you must wear this if you're to return home, sir," he said. "Allow me to carry the shells for you." The contents of Bobby's hat instantly disappeared into one of his pockets, and the hat was placed on the child's head.

"Are you sure you're not the silkie?" asked Bobby.

"I don't know. I might be anything. Who is he?"

"It's a child's story," said Prudence. "An old tale that seals turn into men at night to visit the land; they're called silkies."

"You can tell if you see a seal with blue eyes that he's really a man," explained Bobby, earnestly. "They come to shore and marry real ladies, you know, and steal their hearts, but they always abandon them and their babies, and go back to the sea in the end."

"I see," said the man. "Dashing, of course, but rather thoughtless of them." He turned to Prudence and gently disengaged himself. "I believe I can manage now, angel. But thanks for the assistance. It felt wonderful. If I thought it would always result in your warm hand at my waist and my arm around your enchanting shoulders, I would happily suffer shipwreck every day."

Prudence looked up at him. He was too pale and struggling not to shiver, but he didn't seem in any further need of help. "And if I thought for one moment that you might be taking advantage of me, sir," she said. "I should wish that you had drowned."

His answer was a charming smile. "Angel, you are too severe. For so would I."

Bobby let go of his hand and ran ahead of them toward a track that led up from the beach. A stout, respectable lady stood there shielding her face with her hand.

"Look, Mrs. MacEwen!" cried Bobby. "We have found a man!"

Prudence changed her dress, and vigorously sponged away the sand at the hem and the marks of saltwater from her contact with the man's body. She wished she could as easily scrub away these uncomfortable feelings that she couldn't understand. How could a man in danger of dying of exposure offer all that absurd, meaningless gallantry? And to her, of all people! She glanced at herself in the mirror. Miss Prudence Drake wasn't pretty. Everything about her was nondescript. Her coloring was altogether too washed-out and pale, even her straw-blond hair—it had none of Bobby's golden lights. She was a governess, for heaven's sake. And she had problems of her own.

Half an hour later, Prudence sat in the drawing room while Mr. and Mrs. MacEwen tried to decide what to do with the fellow who had been so inconsiderate as to wash himself up on their beach. Bobby had been sent to the nursery, and the stranger had been allowed to sit in the kitchen, warm himself, and take some refreshment, while the housemaid hovered over him and no doubt happily returned his outlandish flirtation.

"I cannot think that it is perfectly respectable to be found on a beach," said Mrs. MacEwen, tapping her fingers on the arm of the sofa.

"It is a villainous, rascally way to be found, to be sure." Mr. MacEwen examined his pipe and poked in the bowl with a wire.

"I don't like it, Mr. MacEwen. And the man comes from France, sir, where that evil Napoleon was just defeated last year. Let us give the fellow a shilling and send him on his way."

"Yet his speech is very elegant." Mr. MacEwen knocked the pipe against the edge of the grate.

"Fancy words are all very well, but any jackanapes can learn to ape his betters. Look at his appearance! No gentleman ever wore such clothing. It is that of any rough sailor!"

"It is most distressful, indeed."

"And he says he does not know who he is. How can anyone not know their own name?"

"No one but a scoundrel, Mrs. MacEwen, no doubt at all."

"If the fellow ever had anything finer in his background, he has come down in the world."

"An excellent supposition, Mrs. MacEwen. Fled creditors, most like, or the law."

"Oh, good gracious! You do not think he is a criminal?" Mrs. MacEwen turned to Prudence. "How could you bring him here, Miss Drake? When you and Bobby are hiding at the risk of your very lives. That is enough, surely, without threatening all of us with an English vagabond found on the beach!''

''I had no wish to find him, Mrs. MacEwen,'' said Prudence, coloring a little. ''I am very sensible of your kindness in sheltering Bobby and me. Yet I believe the man has had a gentleman's education.''

''Has he, by God?'' Mr. MacEwen began to fill the pipe with fresh tobacco. ''How do you know?''

''He talked about things.'' Even to Prudence's own ears, it sounded lame.

''Then he is a gentleman who has disgraced himself and makes his own way. You mark my words. There is no more dangerous type! Forgotten his name indeed! I never heard such fustian! Remembers it all too well and is afraid we'll have heard ill of it, I'll be bound. Let him have his meal and be gone from here!''

''Yet he's a likely-looking lad,'' said Mr. MacEwen. ''I have given him one of my shirts. You'll have no objection to my giving the lad an old shirt, Mrs. MacEwen?''

She looked up and caught his merry eye. He was teasing her. Mrs. MacEwen frowned. ''That is no more than Christian charity, husband.''

''Nor a bed in the stable for tonight? He isn't strong enough yet, I'll warrant, to be taking to the high road. Besides, what if he was a peer's son or an honorable man with a family, and we turned him out of doors on a cold night?''

''If you lock the house up tight, there'd be no danger in letting him lodge in the stable, I suppose.''

''And tomorrow he can do a little work for his supper. Maybe by then he'll have recalled his name. If it's a good one, there might be a reward in it.''

''Very well, sir,'' said Mrs. MacEwen, ''but on your own head be it if we're all found murdered in our beds.''

''What do you say, Miss Drake? You are very quiet. What

shall we do about this flotsam or jetsam? Shall we shelter this foundling of yours from the sea?''

Prudence looked at the round, kindly face, wreathed now in tobacco smoke, and smiled. ''As my father always said of you, Mr. MacEwen, he never had a friend less likely to follow anyone else's counsel. You were kind enough to give shelter to Bobby and me, when I turned up like a beggar at the door. I believe you have made up your mind to keep him, whatever I might say.''

''And so he has, Prudence,'' said Mrs. MacEwen, wagging her finger. ''So he has. But what time have we for strangers when we have your problem on our hands? What about that, Mr. MacEwen? What if this black lord comes here after wee Bobby?''

''Oh, that can't happen,'' said Prudence with a great deal more conviction than she felt. ''How could Lord Belham possibly find us here?''

Chapter 2

"Devil take it, Ryder. What a damnable, bloody, God-for-saken country! How much longer, for pity's sake?"

The carriage moved along the rutted track like a March hare, now stopping, now leaping ahead with a jolt. The man inside leaned his head back against the squabs and continued to curse with considerable invention.

"I believe the last milestone indicated three more miles, my lord," replied his secretary.

My lord hammered with his cane, and the carriage stopped. "Then I shall walk to Dunraven from here," he said. "Another hour more or less will not make any damned difference to the life of a five-year-old boy. I will probably arrive before you, but if not, tell the countess she may expect me."

"Yes, my lord," said Ryder as his lordship stepped from the carriage.

The peaks on each side of the road sparkled with whiteness. Above them the sky blazed a clear, bright blue. Under the sudden warmth of the sun, rivulets of water were beginning to run out from beneath the snow, making little brown channels across the heather. The man ignored the mud beneath his boots and strode away up the road. The horses nickered after his retreating figure, then the coachman gave them the signal and the carriage lurched forward once again.

The gates of Dunraven Castle were closed. He thundered for some time at the huge oak doors which blocked the entrance. Eventually a wizened head peered over the battlements, and a frail fist was shaken at him.

"Get awa' yon! Get awa' frae the yetts! Vagabonds are nae welcome here!"

"For God's sake, man," said his lordship with the icy certainty of rank and privilege. "I am the Marquess of Belham and the Dowager Countess of Dunraven is not only expecting me, she is also my aunt. The present Lord Dunraven, moreover, has just become my ward. If you do not open these gates, I shall burn them down."

The owner of the white hair peered down for a moment. The dark-visaged fellow below him seemed to have a very business-like pistol in one hand. From a pocket he produced a little flask of powder. Evidently he meant what he said. "Dinna fash yoursel'!" said the retainer. "I'm an auld body. Be patient."

Fifteen minutes later, Lord Belham found himself face-to-face with Lady Dunraven. She seemed to be of a similar age to her servant at the gate, but there was no mistaking that she came from a long line of blue blood. Dressed in black crepe, she sat on a chair which boasted the dimensions of a throne and glared up at her visitor with unrestrained animosity. Her white lace cap crowned her head as brightly as the pure snows crowned the venerable peaks of Beinn Mhanach.

"So, Marquess," she said. "You have come to claim the child."

"Might I sit, Countess?" asked Lord Belham. "I have come some distance."

"Hah! To think that when my husband's sister married your father, it was seen to be a grand match! It is not my custom to have black rakes and villains sit at my fireside, sir!"

"Then I shall be happy to stand, of course." He crossed to the small peat fire that smoldered sullenly in the hearth, and held out his hands. Firelight glinted on a large gold signet ring on his finger. The tiny gleam of warmth seemed to be entirely swallowed up by the cavernous, feudal chimney and the vast reaches of the stone-vaulted ceiling. "It was your son's last wish before he died that the care of young Robert come to me."

There was silence for a moment. They were both looking at a portrait which hung over the fireplace. A young man smiled back at them above a small plaque which identified him as Henry, fourth Earl of Dunraven.

"Henry died too young!" snapped Lady Dunraven.

"But he put his desire for the guardianship in writing with the full blessing of the law. We are both bound by it."

"How was Henry to know the bad blood that runs through Belham like the stink in the gutter of the wynd? I don't doubt it was your infernal influence that undermined his health with drinking and bad women after his wife died—my only son! *You* led him to an early grave. Now, should anything happen to the child, you are heir to both lines, aren't you?"

Lord Belham turned from the fire and looked down at her. His mouth was set in something very close to a sneer. "And why, pray, should anything happen to Robert? The little Lord Dunraven isn't sickly, is he?"

"He enjoys very robust health, sir. But the life of a five-year-old hangs by a slender enough thread."

"I suppose it does," said the marquess dryly. "Might I see the child and judge for myself?"

"He is not here." It was said with considerable triumph.

"I thought Henry sent the boy here after Christmas? When he knew he was dying?"

"So he did."

"Then where, pray, is Robert now?"

The Dowager Countess stood up. She held out one scrawny hand and shook a finger at the marquess's face. "Where you can't get to him, sir! Where he can grow up into his estates without hindrance. Where there is no profligate gambler and rake to threaten his health and his innocence. I have sent the child away, sir!''

''Oh, God!'' said Lord Belham with biting sarcasm. ''Then how the hell am I supposed to get my hands on his inheritance?''

''Not by doing harm to my little grandson, sir!''

''Madam, whether I am the blackest villain in Britain or not, do you really think I plan to murder the fifth Lord Dunraven?''

She pursed her lips. ''Neglect would be enough, sir. Neglect and a little carelessness. Then you might turn me out of here, sell up Dunraven Castle, and pay off your gaming debts and your mistress's duns. It would be a small thing to snap the thread that holds life in my little Bobby.''

If Lord Belham was angry at such an outrageous suggestion, it didn't show in his face. He walked up and down for a moment as if considering his next course of action.

''Very well,'' he said at last. ''You win. I have pressing affairs in London, and I don't have time for this. Keep your grandson where you will, madam. I wash my hands of it.''

He gave her a stiff bow and left the room. In the castle courtyard stood his carriage, the rampant eagles of Belham emblazoned on the door panel. Lord Belham stopped and looked at them for a moment, then he ran his long fingers over the painting and smiled.

''Wherever you go destruction flies with you,'' he said under his breath to the rearing eagles. ''Unspeakable vice smolders in your fiery glance. So sweet Lady Dunraven is too smart to let you get your depraved and bloody claws into her little grandson. What a pity!'' He grinned up at his coachman. ''We are to turn around, George; to hell with the horses.''

''But they're being baited, my lord,'' replied the coachman.

Lord Belham laughed. ''Since the shafts stand empty, so I see, sir. But once my steeds from Hades have had their supper, we head back to England.''

The coachman scratched his head and nodded. What was

one more queer start from the marquess? Meanwhile his master
walked into the stable. The secretary was overseeing the feeding
and grooming of the team.

Ryder raised his brows at the sight of Belham's face. "Does
Lady Dunraven not part willingly with her grandson, my lord?"

The marquess's voice was very soft. "We retreat, Ryder,
defeated and without the child. She has sent him away. But
leave a man here to discreetly ask about among the servants,
will you? Have him pursue the runaway and report directly
back to me. The boy must have had a nursemaid with him, or
a governess, or tutor. He or she will have friends somewhere,
connections. Scotland isn't so big. I want little Lord Dunraven
found. Is that clear?"

Ryder bowed his head. "Perfectly, my lord," he said.

The next day brought a fine mist, which enveloped the
MacEwens' household in a soft, white embrace. Prudence
sorted through the mending and the wash, and then went up to
the nursery to find Bobby and give him his breakfast. The
room had been bedroom, schoolroom, and playroom for all the
MacEwens' children, and it was still filled with toys and books.
A fire burned merrily in the grate, and a maid was polishing
the brass around the fender. Bobby's bedclothes were tumbled
about, but he was not there. Prudence knew a moment of sheer
panic. *Lord Belham had broken in during the night and spirited
the child away!* Then she dropped into one of the battered old
chairs and caught her breath at her own absurdity.

"Bobby is in the stables, ma'am," said the maid, stopping
her polishing and giving Prudence a merry smile. "He's very
taken with the drowned gentleman."

"The drowned gentleman? Oh, no! I mean, of course! Thank
you."

Prudence hurried back down the stairs and out into the yard.

She had hardly forgotten the man she had found on the beach.
In fact, she had dreamt about him: he had come swimming into

her room in the sleek fur coat of a seal, sinuous, graceful, and with the wild thyme-laden, salt-rich scent of the Outer Isles about him. Then the fur dropped away leaving him standing gloriously naked at the foot of her bed. He had held out a hand to her and laughed. She had woken, her heart beating too fast, to stare with the most absurd consternation into the cold dark of her little room. Thank goodness the dream image had been so vague and shadowed! What on earth would Papa have thought of his calm and capable daughter, if he knew that she had such dreams?

The thick mist cloaked the buildings and wreathed silently around the chimneys, so that the peaks which rose up behind the house had disappeared. A stranger would never have known that the MacEwens lived between the sea and the mountains, except for the steady murmur of the surf, sounding muffled and ghostly in the distance. But a bright light shone from the stable. There was a little harness room at one end of the old building, with a stove and a bed. The light was coming from there.

Prudence walked up to the door and looked in. Next to the stove was a broad patch of warm tile. Bobby was kneeling there in his muslin suit. Since he had dressed himself, the buttons were mismatched. The man from the beach squatted in his shirtsleeves on the floor beside him. His dark head was tilted as he listened to the child's earnest voice. The little boy was entirely absorbed.

"This is the silkie. See here. He comes out of the sea and leaves his fur coat. Then he looks like a man." Bobby pushed a little scrap of fur up a beach he had made from his collection of shells. A twig which had been wrapped in the fur emerged to play the part of the man. "His home is the sea and he's the strongest man there is. And he's lord of the fishes and the whales and the seals."

"And do the ladies admire him for that?" asked the man from the beach quite seriously.

"They fall in love with him because he's comely," said Bobby.

"But can his lady never keep him by her side?"

Bobby picked up a shell and moved it very deliberately over the scrap of fur. "Only if she can find his fur coat and burn it. Then he's a man forever and she can marry him. But if she doesn't do it right, he dies."

"Oh, dear. Then it's rather a risky venture to try and wed him, isn't it?"

"Well, she doesn't always marry him," said Bobby.

"Ah. Do the lady and the silkie have children?"

Bobby clutched at the little stick figure. His blond head was bent so that his face couldn't be seen. "If there's a little boy, like me, his father will come for him one day and take him, and teach him how to swim in the ocean. But till then the silkie's swimming forever out in the cold sea between Mull and the Skerries. I wish he would come! I wish he would come soon!"

Prudence could hardly hear the man's voice, it was so gentle. "Perhaps the silkie has to swim out there in the wild Atlantic, for it's his nature and he cannot help it. But it must be very hard for his little boy who is left behind."

"It is," said Bobby. "Very hard."

"I should very much like to meet a silkie. Wouldn't you?"

Bobby looked up at him, eyes shining with unshed tears. "They never admit who they are," he replied.

The man said something in the child's ear too quiet for her to hear. And Bobby smiled, with a sudden rush of faith lighting up his face like a lamp.

"It's time for your breakfast, Bobby," said Prudence. She felt like a brute to interrupt, but she must!

The harebell eyes glanced up at her. He looked very different now he was bathed and dry: in spite of his simple clothes, every inch a gentleman and extremely self-possessed. "Why, Miss Drake! Breakfast sounds like an excellent idea. But what celestial fare do angels eat? Shall we dine on ambrosia and honeydew?''

Bobby ran up to her and flung his arms around her skirt. ''I want eggs,'' he said.

Prudence hugged him, and watched as he ran across the yard back to the house. She glanced down at the man, now sprawling comfortably on the tile with his back to the wall. He grinned insolently up at her with a bravado that dared her to object. ''Whoever you are, please don't do this!'' she asked. ''It's not fair to Bobby!''

''What isn't fair?''

''That you should try to charm him! What if he begins to care about you? He lost his mother when he was too little to remember, and his father has been dead only a few months. Why should Bobby matter to you? How long do you plan to stay here: a few days, a week?''

He dropped his dark lashes over the deep blue eyes for a moment. ''I assure you I shall not do Bobby any harm. I offer him a little friendship, that's all.''

''A friendship! Is that what I saw happening here? He is already besotted with you! Good heavens, sir. You are only a passing encounter in this child's life! It's unconscionable that you should encourage him to care about you, then leave him bereft once again.''

A warm glow of light from the stove flickered lovingly over the bones of his face. ''Then you don't think that strangers should offer love to each other, even briefly? What a cold-hearted world you would like to inhabit, angel!''

''Love? That is an emotion which grows out of knowing a person well. By definition strangers can't love each other.''

He lifted his lashes and gazed straight at her. There was a treasury of lightly-felt mockery there. ''Not even in Christian charity?''

It only made Prudence angry.

''We are not talking about Christian charity,'' she snapped. ''We are talking about wantonly engaging deep, personal feelings which can't be returned. Which you have no intention of returning."

"How can you know what my intentions are?" The laughter disappeared from his face. "As it happens, I don't agree with you at all. I think the world is a lonely enough place, so lonely that the people in it should love each other whenever they can, even if for only one day, or for only one night, as long as they're honest with each other. Caring and sympathy are the only feelings that should never be withheld. Why the devil should Bobby not find some temporary comfort in me if he wants to? And if the child gives me his trust, I promise you I shan't betray it."

Prudence was truly angry now. "This is arrant nonsense, sir, and you know it. Out of vanity, you're letting him form an attachment which you will break as carelessly as a crust of bread, leaving him bereft once again. I would be very grateful, therefore, if you would keep your distance from him!"

"Sorry, angel. I don't agree and I won't do it."

"Sir, Bobby is in my charge! I think I know what's best for him."

In a remarkably smooth movement, he stood up and walked boldly up to her. His voice had become tight, as if he bit back anger. "No, you don't, Miss Drake. You don't even know what's best for yourself. Why the devil do you pull your hair back so severely? It makes you look like a nun. Is that the idea?"

Prudence felt the color rise in her neck. "We're not talking about me, sir. We're discussing the child."

"You may be talking about the child, sweet creature of heaven. I am talking about you. Are you honest? I don't know who I am and I freely admit it. Do you know who you are?"

"I am Prudence Drake," she said, and hated to hear the frantic, unsure tones in her own voice.

"And who is that? A governess, very prim, very proper. Have you ever let your hair down?"

"What do you mean? Of course!"

''No, I don't mean when you comb it out at night and instantly trap it back into a severe plait again. I mean: have you ever let your hair down and run along a beach in your shift, or pulled out your pins because a warm breeze is blowing from the summer sky and you want to feel long tendrils caress your bare arms. Have you ever let down your hair in front of a man?''

A flood of uncomfortable heat coursed through her body.''Oh, good gracious! This is absurd and outrageous, sir!''

And suddenly he grinned and the odd mood was broken. ''Yes, it is, isn't it? Yet I would like to know, though I have no idea why. Forgive me, Miss Drake. I am just a scoundrel from the sea. But when you suggest that I might do some harm to the child, it makes me forget my better manners. I beg you will accept my most humble apology if my talk runs wilder than my more honorable intentions.''

He gave her a glance so full of contrition that Prudence felt her indignation die away, although her uncertainty and the flush in her blood remained. Truly, how could this man do Bobby any damage? Was she—ignobly—jealous, that he had so very simply and quickly earned the child's confidence? ''Very well,'' she said. ''I realize that all this must be very hard for you, too. Not knowing who you are or whence you came. From where do you suppose you have acquired your ease with children? Do you think you have a little boy of your own?''

''Good God! No! At least, I don't believe I do.'' He looked at his hands and spread the fingers. Prudence noticed the shape of them: long, slim, square-ended. They were naturally elegant hands, and undamaged but for some scrapes and blisters of recent origin. Hardly the hands of a sailor. ''I am not wearing a wedding ring,'' he said. Then he looked at her, and Prudence knew that even if he had asked for forgiveness, she was not entirely forgiven. ''Not that the lack of a wedding precludes bastards, of course.''

Prudence went scarlet with chagrin. He was baiting her deliberately! She refused to rise to it. ''Perhaps you have brothers and sisters, then.''

''John,'' he said suddenly. And his expression became open, touched with genuine revelation. ''I have a little brother, John. And sisters.''

''What are their names?''

''Matty, and—'' He stopped and looked blankly at her. ''I'm not sure if that's right.''

''Matty who? John who?''

''I don't know.''

''What other names come to mind, sir?''

He stepped over to the stove and opened it. The hot glare cast red light over his high cheekbones and touched sparks of fire in his black hair as he loaded more fuel. ''Helena.'' The word escaped with his breath, soft as a caress.

''Who's Helena? A little sister?''

''I don't think so!'' He ran a hand over his face. ''Dear God, how absurd this makes me.''

And Prudence felt a surprising rush of compassion. Dear Lord, whatever he was, what a frightful predicament this must be for him! ''You must choose a name for yourself. We can't go on referring to you as the 'drowned gentleman', can we?''

''Very well, what do you suggest?''

''You said your name began with 'P', or maybe 'H'. Peter, Paul?''

He grinned at her. ''Percival, Philoctetes? Hector, Hyperion, Hercules? Polycrates, Plutarch? Ah, Miss Drake, how nice to see you smile again. Hannibal?''

Prudence attempted to force her brows together in a frown. ''Percy, Philip, Patrick? Hugh, Henry, Harold? Does nothing ring a bell?''

''Henry, Harold—the bell begins to tinkle somehow. Oh, dear God, of course! 'Harry the fifth's the man, I speak the truth.' I believe I am named after Prince Hal, angel. 'Hal' rings a distinct bell. In fact I believe it rings a carillon, enough to shake the bell tower and deafen the campanologist. You may call me Hal, Miss Drake, if you please.''

"Hal who?"

But his expression closed, whether from desperation, frustration, or deliberate concealment, Prudence couldn't say.

"Now that's another question for another time, don't you think? Like Tantalus, I'm starving, Miss Drake. Allow me to escort you to breakfast.''

The mist did not entirely burn off until the next week, when at last bright sunshine streamed unhindered into the stone courtyard. Prudence sat by the nursery fire mending clothes as Bobby played with a stout pile of blocks. She couldn't stop thinking about Hal. There seemed to be nothing she could do about him and Bobby, and her hostility to him only resulted in Hal's teasing her unmercifully. So she had avoided him and done her best to keep Bobby out of his way. For an entire week. And for an entire week, she had not been able to stop thinking about him. Every day she would hear his laughter and the ring of his boots. She would see his eyes boldly watching her at every mealtime, even though she kept her gaze firmly on her plate. And she had dreamt about him again—every night for a week. It seemed like an unpardonable treachery to herself, and filled her with fury.

When she had stepped out into the yard first thing that morning, she had found him sitting on the mounting block, the sun sparkling off his dark hair. Very much at ease, Hal was wearing one of Mr. MacEwen's old tan coats, his long legs stretched before him, vigorously applying polish to his boots. Prudence had tried to ignore him, but as she walked past he looked up and said, " 'And is not my hostess of the tavern a most sweet wench?' / 'As the honey of Hybla, my old lad of the castle. And is not a buff jerkin a most sweet robe of durance?' "

Which was Prince Hal and Falstaff, wasn't it? All those evenings spent reading aloud with her father and the other children around the fire came flooding back. " 'How now, how now,' " answered Prudence without thinking that even Shakespeare could use the crudest of language, " 'mad wag! What, in thy quips and thy quiddities? What a plague have I to do with a buff jerkin?' "

She had asked for it, of course. Hal grinned and replied, " 'Why, what a pox have I to do with my hostess of the tavern?' "

Which had caused Prudence to flush unhappily with color and flee back inside. Yet Hal had so easily insinuated himself into the household! He seemed to have a natural gift with children, and in spite of her attempt to warn him off, had offered every day a feast of games and stories which enchanted Bobby. Mr. MacEwen happily announced he had found a willing hand to help him with his work, and Mrs. MacEwen had been thoroughly charmed out of all of her dire suspicions. So by the time the sun returned to Argyleshire, Hal had taken over the room in the stables as if he owned it, and had the run of the Manse as if he were an honored and trusted guest.

Prudence laid down her sewing and walked restlessly to the window. Dear God, he could be anyone! But it was becoming clear what he was not: he was not an ordinary, comfortable person. He wasn't safe, or reassuring, or easy to understand. Hal was not like the boys or young men she had known while she was growing up, the respectable daughter of a small-town Scottish doctor, and he was nothing like her brothers.

As she stood staring blindly out over the sleeping mountains of Lorne, there was the sudden shattering sound of gunfire— two shots in quick succession followed by the unmistakable thud of lead balls hitting a soft target. Prudence whirled around.

But faster than she could react, Bobby jumped up, the blocks tumbling unheeded behind him, and ran from the room.

Chapter 3

Prudence found Bobby hanging onto the five-barred gate that led from the courtyard into the sheep runs behind the workshop.

"Look, Miss Drake!" called Bobby. "Mr. MacEwen has a new pistol ready. And Hal is trying it out."

Prudence watched as Hal smoothly primed and reloaded a pair of dueling pistols that Mr. MacEwen had finished making earlier that week. Hal was in his shirt sleeves, with the cuffs rolled back to show his strong, lean forearms and clean-boned wrists. He wore no cravat. Instead the rough work shirt lay open at the neck, the collar carelessly twisted. His hair was a little long. It overhung the high collar by several inches at the back. "They're a little short in the barrel for my taste," he said seriously to the older man. "But they don't lack for accuracy, and the trigger approaches the dishonorable in sensitivity! A deuced fine piece of work, sir."

With a pistol in each hand, Hal spun toward a paper target which Mr. MacEwen had fixed to the side of his haystack. Almost casually he lifted each arm in turn, and fired.

"Another two bull's-eyes!" squealed Bobby.

Prudence knew very little of firearms, even though there had been a gunsmith living at Dunraven. But she could recognize expertise when she saw it. A stunning proficiency lay in every line of Hal's figure: in the careless, masculine stance; the perfect line from shoulder to hand and along the barrel; the passion which concentrated his expression. The target had been neatly punctured four times in the exact center. Hal was a dead shot—and with either hand, for heaven's sake! Prudence bent and caught Bobby around the shoulders. This could ruinously increase his hero-worship for the stranger! Only the promise of warm scones in the kitchen was enough to make the child jump from the gate and run inside, out of harm's way. She watched him go with unrepentant relief.

"An awkward skill, don't you think, angel?" asked Hal.

Prudence turned and looked up at him. He had left Mr. MacEwen examining the pistols, and walked over to her. Sunlight glanced off the ruffled dark hair over his forehead, casting shadows on the clean bone-structure of his face.

"What do you mean?"

"That I should show such a nasty and thorough proficiency with firearms." Hal looked thoughtfully at the target. "What do you think that reveals about me?"

"I don't know," said Prudence. "Most gentlemen shoot, don't they?" She felt foolish and inadequate in the face of his easy confidence.

He grinned. "Well, thank goodness for that! But the real question is, what kind of gentlemen?"

"What do you mean?"

"A gentleman may enjoy shooting at his pheasant, or even possibly at his neighbor if they should quarrel, but he's generally not going to devote himself so exclusively to mayhem with a pistol that he would bother to devote unending hours of practice to it. And that"—He nodded at the target—"Speaks to an unhealthy amount of time in a shooting range." He laughed suddenly. "Perhaps I am a gentleman of the road!"

Prudence sensed danger as clearly as if he pointed a pistol at her heart. "Oh, goodness! You think you are a highwayman?"

"We can't be sure, can we? Do you think I am dedicated to a life of crime, angel?"

"Please, don't," said Prudence a little desperately.

He looked down at her. "Don't what?"

"Don't call me *angel!* It's silly and inappropriate."

He touched her hair lightly where it swept over her ear into her severe bun. "No, it's not!" It was the briefest, most impersonal of caresses and his hand dropped immediately, but she felt the effect of the contact shake her to the knees.

Prudence colored. "And improper and overly familiar."

"Is it? But a highwayman is used to treating ladies with cavalier gallantry, isn't he? Didn't the infamous Claude Du Vall dance a coranto with a lady victim on Hounslow Heath? To the music of her own flageolet, no less."

"How could she play if she was dancing, sir?" asked Prudence sternly.

The blue eyes gravely surveyed her. Yet beneath the seriousness of his expression, laughter bubbled like water boiling below a pan lid. "The tale doesn't say. Perhaps her maid was also proficient at the flute. And then he took her jewels, her husband's money, and her heart, of course. 'Du Vall, the ladies' joy; Du Vall the ladies' grief'—he ended up in Newgate."

"A proper end for such a villain." Prudence ran one hand firmly over her hair as if to brush away the lingering trace of his hand.

> " 'Thither came ladies from all parts
> To offer up close prisoners' hearts
> which he received as tribute due,
> And made them yield up—' "

Hal stopped and grinned. "Alas, it becomes just a little indelicate, Miss Drake."

She could see that he was teasing her. It left her a little lost, but she met the challenge with one of her own. "My father was a doctor. I am not foolish, nor a shrinking violet. You cannot stop now."

He laughed. " 'And made them yield up love and honor too.' But only symbolically, we must assume, for the gallant Du Vall would have been in chains. Of course, he could have kissed them—if they cooperated."

Prudence hated her own betraying high color. He must think her a bluenose. "And then what happened?"

"He was hanged at Tyburn on January 21, 1670. Do you suppose I am one of his company, and a wanted man?"

"I don't care who you are, sir, as long as you're not a danger to Bobby and me." Prudence wished fervently that he had never come to Argyleshire and that he would go away soon.

"Why should anything or anyone be a danger to you and a five-year-old boy, Miss Drake?" asked Hal.

Fortunately she did not have to reply. There was a rattle of wheels coming up the driveway. Mrs. MacEwen and her maid were returning from town with the shopping. Their gig stopped at the gate. Mrs. MacEwen smiled at Prudence as Mr. MacEwen came up to join them, but there was a genuine worry in her eyes.

"We have a problem, Mr. MacEwen," she said. She was avoiding Hal's gaze. "That report about the ship from France that went down was, by the blessing of Providence, false. Not that I can think it right that our ships should visit France at all. Be that as it may, she was driven north by the storm, but she came into harbor three days ago. Battered and torn, Mr. MacEwen, but with all hands—and all passengers, not a one lost overboard."

"Did she?" asked Mr. MacEwen thoughtfully.

Now everyone was looking at Hal. He leaned back against the gate and folded his arms across his chest. "How very awkward, to be sure," he said. "In that case, where did I come from?"

"Which is the very question that I would like answered,

sir,'' said Mrs. MacEwen. Her voice was edged with disappointment. She had fallen very completely for the handsome young stranger. ''For unless you came from a shipwreck, it seems very ill-mannered to be found half-drowned on the beach.'' She whipped up her horse and drove on into the yard.

''Alas,'' said Hal with a quiet laugh. '' 'Methinks he hath no drowning mark upon him; his complexion is perfect gallows.' ''

Prudence glanced up at him. He seemed only amused by this disastrous news. How could he be so cavalier about it? She turned away to follow Mrs. MacEwen to the house. And it said absolutely nothing about him that he knew Shakespeare. Who wouldn't recognize *The Tempest?*

''So, we have a conundrum,'' said Mr. MacEwen with a considered look at his guest. ''There are no other ships reported missing.''

'' 'This is as strange a maze as e'er men trod,' '' continued Hal lightly. ''If I was not lost from that French ship, then how did I end up here?''

Mr. MacEwen glanced down at the pistol in his hand. The beauty of it moved him as it always did, and this young fellow understood that, understood his passion for perfecting the craft, for inventing the ultimate improvement. He made up his mind in that instant. ''Never mind, lad. We'll get to the bottom of it soon enough. And in the meantime, how would you like to work for me on a permanent basis? You seem to have a very pretty knowledge of firearms. And though I'm supposed to be a retired man and the pistols only a hobby now, I have some experimental work in hand that might interest you. There are some ideas about for a whole new mechanism that'll make our flintlocks seem as outdated as the matchlock.''

''I cannot commit to anything, Mr. MacEwen.'' Hal was suddenly serious. ''I know you will allow me that under the circumstances. But I will freely help you as long as I'm here.''

His glance followed Prudence as she walked into the house. "Miss Drake is not too happy about my presence."

"You would not stay for one more day if I thought you were making her truly uncomfortable," said Mr. MacEwen. "But don't mind her, Hal. She's just nervous about the lad."

"Would you think me impertinent if I ask why they are here? It seems a little unusual. I gather that Bobby is an orphan?"

"Aye, poor lad. Prudence is all he has left, but for an old granny. I knew Miss Drake's father, sir. We're old family friends. She just takes the boy for a little holiday by the sea, away from the *cailleach.*"

Hal raised a brow. And in that moment Mr. MacEwen knew with certainty what he had suspected from the start. This young fellow might be lost and bewildered as to his place in the world, but when he came into his senses, he was going to discover that it was a very high place indeed. Nobody but a lord, and one who had gone through the cruel rigors of an English public school, could raise one brow in quite such an insolent way while pretending it was merely curiosity.

But Mr. MacEwen was not to be intimidated. *"Cailleach,"* he repeated. "Old woman, beldam, the lad's grandmother. Miss Drake is in her employ, sir. There's no mystery to it."

"No," said Hal innocently. "I didn't suppose for one moment that there was. Does Miss Drake have a large family of her own?"

"She has one brother at sea and another in India; a sister who teaches school in Edinburgh and one married in Wiltshire. That's all."

"Then her parents are not alive?"

But Mr. MacEwen would give nothing else away. "No, they are not," he said. And he began to talk about guns.

Mrs. MacEwen's maid met Prudence in the hall. Her face was filled with honest concern.

"I didn't like to say anything in front of that Hal fellow,

ma'am,'' she said. ''And I've not told Mr. or Mrs. MacEwen, not wanting to worry the decent bodies, but you asked me to keep out a weather eye and I thought I should tell you. A man has been seen in the village, a stranger to these parts. He had an eye-patch, like an old soldier or a villain. He asked after newcomers to the area, asked if anyone had seen an unfamiliar gentleman, but when it was mentioned that you were the only stranger here, he seemed to know your description already: yellow hair, hazel eyes, less pretty than average—and he had a complete portrayal of the boy.''

''Oh, dear heavens,'' said Prudence as her heart seemed to stop in her breast. She sat down.

Months earlier that anyone would have thought possible, they were run to earth.

Bobby did not want to go. He did not want to leave the silkie man that he had found on the beach. This was why! This was why she had begged Hal not to engage the child's affections! Bobby cried piteously into Prudence's shoulder as she rocked him in her arms in the dark nursery. She had already packed up their few bags and made up a little package of food from the kitchen. And of course she had the purse full of coin that Lady Dunraven had given her. Dear heavens, Bobby had lost everything in his short life: his mother when he was two; his father, wasting away from consumption only the previous winter; his home in London, then at Dunraven; and now he must lose the kindly company of Mr. and Mrs. MacEwen— and must be torn away from the unprincipled man he had befriended. The child had only herself, a hired governess, between him and desolation.

She sang a snatch of the song about the silkie under her breath. ''He's taken out a purse of gold and laid it on the nurse's knee / Give to me my bonny wee son and take ye up your nurse's fee.'' It was more of a croon than a song, but when she reached the next verse—''I will fetch my bonny wee son and teach him how to swim the foam''—Bobby objected.

''Don't sing it! Hal will teach me,'' wailed Bobby. ''I want Hal! I found him on the beach. He came here for me.''

His sobs wracked her heart.

Eventually Bobby fell damply asleep. The rest of the household had gone to bed. Silently she slipped down to the stable yard and harnessed up the governess cart. A short note to Mr. and Mrs. MacEwen lay on the mantel. Prudence would not involve them further. It was a note they could show to Black Belham himself if he came here. It would absolve the MacEwens of blame, and prove that her destination was unknown to them. She would send a letter to Lady Dunraven from Glasgow: she was pursuing their second plan now. Another trip packed the cart with the bags and provisions. Then she carried the sleeping child down through the silent house and tucked him into the little bed of blankets she had made in the cart.

As they passed Hal's window, the horse's hoofs made what seemed a thunderous clangor in the stone yard. Prudence felt frantic with fear. She ought to have muffled the nag's feet with sackcloth! Bobby stirred and whimpered a little, but did not wake up. With one glance at the silent house and dark stable, Prudence tried to lead the horse toward the gate. It stopped stubbornly, not wanting to leave its companions in the stable.

And Hal? Had the sound of the hooves woken him yet?

Prudence tiptoed to the little room at the end of the stable and peeked in the window. On a cot against the far wall Hal lay as abandoned as he had seemed on the beach. His hair was jet black against the pillow. Deep shadows lay under his jaw and beneath the strong line of his neck where it met his collar bone. In sleep he looked younger, but every bit as dangerous. Prudence noticed with the smallest shock that Hal did not seem to be wearing a nightshirt. The strong curve of his naked shoulder disappeared under the sheet. It seemed a dishonorable and underhanded thing, even to check on him, but thank God he still slept.

Prudence went back to the recalcitrant animal and took it firmly by the bit. Like the morning rooster shattering the dawn, the horse whinnied. There was an answering chorus of equine leave-taking from the stable. Oh, God! Everyone would wake up. Mr. MacEwen would try to stop her. Who could really believe that a marquess would be prepared to murder a child for his inheritance? Mr. MacEwen would insist that she stay, the daughter of his old friend; he would think he could protect her.

With some frantic tugging and pulling, Prudence eventually forced the horse to leave the yard. Once they were in the lane, she climbed onto the little box and took up the whip. Now that it had met with a stronger will and left its companions behind, the horse went amiably enough down the lane. Prudence turned its head south. Toward England.

The night was clear and crisp with a high sailing moon; the road frosted and hard. But the day's ruts had become treacherous traps for the wheels. She had gone perhaps five miles and was close to the little stone bridge across the frozen burn, when she realized that the horse had begun to limp. This could be disaster! Prudence climbed from the cart and ran her hand down the horse's legs, just as the moon disappeared behind some great fist of cloud. Black silence streamed about her, the only sound the animal's hot breathing, the only motion the little puffs of steam from its nostrils. She picked up its forefoot. And heard, as chilling as the clutch of a stranger's hand in a dark room, a rustle in the willows beside the road and the distinct sound of footsteps coming her way.

Hal woke instantly when the horses began to whinny. A rush of images raced through his mind. Dear God, he had been dreaming again! A confused jumble of scenes, echoing with broken snatches of rhyme and a far-off sound of screaming. *There was a young fellow who kissed / madame in her shift, but he missed* . . . Ragged glimpses of a charming small courtyard with a trellis covered in white roses; a blur of gaming tables and empty wine bottles and men shouting; a building burning fiercely, its timbers crashing down in sheets of flame; the shadowy faces of women. Some of them seemed very young, barely more than children; some bold-eyed and flirtatious. But only one entangled his emotions in a way which filled him with a longing that he couldn't understand. A beautiful face, calm and clear-eyed, graced by its frame of bright blond hair. She had been saying, "But I don't think I can so easily forgive you," before her features dissolved into the dream. Hal sat up in the bed and ran his hands through his hair. Who the devil was he? Why in Hades couldn't he remember? And what the hell was he doing washed up on a beach in Scotland?

There was the distinct sound of a horse clopping from the courtyard into the lane. Hal sprang naked from the bed and crossed to the window. The moonlight cast its cold light over a slender figure climbing onto the seat of a governess cart. Miss Drake had just shut the gate behind her. *Now, where the devil was she going?* Without hesitation, he flung on his clothes: the shirt that Mr. MacEwen had given him; the serge trousers and reefer jacket that he had been wearing on the beach; his boots, shining now with the daily application of polish. The clothes were as much a mystery to him as the face in the mirror when he shaved in the morning—with a borrowed razor into a stranger's basin. He left the tan jacket that Mr. MacEwen had loaned him in the room, and with a borrowed pen on Mr. MacEwen's paper wrote a short note to his host. Then Hal strode out into the yard and glanced up at the moon. He owned nothing in the world, not even a name.

Prudence let down the horse's foot and stared into the willows. She could see only blackness among the shifting, duplicitous stalks and treacherous leaves. She could hear nothing but the hammering of her own heart. The horse shifted a little and blew through its nostrils. Then the crisp sound of the icy surface giving way beneath boots rang clearly through the night. Rapidly climbing back into the cart, Prudence whipped up the horse. It balked, then lurched forward toward the bridge.

"For God's sake," said a carefree voice. "Your nag is gimpy. Perhaps he has a stone?"

Prudence choked back a scream. Bobby woke up and began to cry. A man stepped out of a small gap in the trees where a footpath from the MacEwen's house ran into the road, and caught the horse's rein near the bit.

Moonlight streamed out again from between the drifting clouds.

"Oh, good gracious!" Prudence's breath was still coming in gasps.

"The night creates monsters," said Hal with a grin. "Fit for fairy tales. But they offer only enchantment to women. Sorry if I scared you, Miss Drake, but this is rather an odd time to take a jaunt around the countryside, isn't it?"

Bobby sat up and wiped his face on his small pudgy hand. Then he beamed. "Hello, Hal," he said. "Are you coming with us?"

Hal smiled at Bobby. "Of course. You didn't think for a moment that you could leave me behind, did you? And I think you need me to see to your horse." He took a small knife from his pocket and efficiently dislodged a stone from the horse's hoof. "There you are, old fellow," he said cheerfully, patting the animal on the neck. Then he grinned up at Prudence and climbed onto the box beside her. Bobby had dropped back into his nest of blankets and, with the ease possible only in a young child, gone straight back to sleep.

"What do you think you're doing?" asked Prudence, choking back her tumult of emotion. For Hal had laid his hand over hers.

"I am taking the reins, dear Miss Drake. Otherwise you will have us all in the ditch."

She pulled her hands away. "You'll do no such thing, sir."

The horse lurched across the road as he felt the tug at the bit.

Hal caught the rein and directed him back. "I shall, indeed. For you are going to get into the back with Bobby and make sure he is covered against the cold, and I am going to be your coachman, guard, and ostler."

Prudence tugged hard and the horse jerked to a halt. "Let me make this clear, sir. I do not want company, yours least of all. I am in something of a hurry and I would be grateful if you would cease these unwanted attentions this instant."

Hal burst out laughing. "Unwanted attentions? Good Lord, angel. I am not trying to kiss you, merely trying to drive the horse."

She knew she was blushing uncomfortably. "But I don't wish it."

"Do you really expect that I shall obey such an absurd desire?"

"A gentleman would," she said stubbornly.

"Ah," said Hal. "And there I think you are wrong. No gentleman would allow a lady to drive alone and unprotected along what is little more than a track in the dark. It is a gentleman's duty to be chivalrous, protective, and helpful to ladies. You shan't deny me the chance to act the knight errant."

"But you don't even know where I am going."

"Well, you would seem to be going south. It lacks only an hour or two to midnight. According to Mrs. MacEwen's maid, who is a fount of information and has filled me in on every detail of daily life in these parts, this is the road to Glasgow. From which noble city coaches leave every morning on their journey to Carlisle, but whence there are no coaches at all going north. Why on earth you should suddenly want to go to Carlisle in the middle of the night, I have no idea, but it's not safe that you should do so with no other company than a child's. Therefore, I am coming too."

"You are not!"

"You can't stop me, angel. Besides, what will you do if the horse goes lame again?"

"But why would you want to come?"

"Why not? I have nowhere else to go, after all."

It wasn't fair. He was using the appalling circumstance of his shipwreck, if that was what really had happened, and the injury which had resulted in his loss of memory, to engage her sympathy. She looked once at his face. He quite obviously knew it, and had no qualms about so manipulating her. But he also looked confident, capable, and commanding. And there was a long, dark road to Glasgow ahead. The presence of a man was reassuring. Or it would be if the man weren't Hal!

"Your predicament isn't my concern, sir," Prudence insisted. "I don't want company, and there's an end of it."

Bobby whimpered and turned over. Prudence glanced back at him; his small white hand lay exposed to the cold air above the cover.

"Alas, but Bobby does. Would you leave him to frostbite in order to nurse your entirely unfounded mistrust? Miss Drake, pray allow me to drive you to Glasgow, or I shall turn this horse around and take you straight back to Mr. and Mrs. MacEwen. In fact, I'm not sure that I shouldn't do so anyway."

"No!" said Prudence. "You cannot, sir! Mr. MacEwen knows why I am gone. He would not try to stop me." It seemed a very small lie, considering what she knew of Black Belham.

"Very well," replied Hal calmly. "Then I will take you south, Miss Drake. I fear that Bobby is getting cold. Will you take care of him, or must I?"

Without remonstrating further, she thrust the reins into Hal's hands and climbed into the back. It need only be until she reached the coaching inn; once she and Bobby were on the public stage they would be safe. And until then perhaps it was foolish to travel alone. After all, Lady Dunraven had sent an escort with her to the MacEwens' house. But how foolish that move had turned out to be! They should have known that it wouldn't be safe for long—that a marquess would be able to discover the name of her father's old friend. Lord Belham had too much to gain from laying hands on his new ward. He would never meekly give up the search.

Prudence gathered Bobby against her breast and wrapped him securely into her own warmth. Within ten minutes she was fast asleep as Hal drove steadily on through the night.

"I am sorry," said the man with the eye-patch. "I know nothing of medicines. I am only asking if there have been strangers seen hereabouts. I have lost my boy, and search for news of him."

It was late in the night, but light still streamed from the tiny window of the bothy. There was a child sick inside, and his father had sent for the doctor.

"Strangers? There is the lady and the wee lad up at the Manse, sir, as you have just described to me yourself," replied the soft Highland voice in the perfect, unaccented English that all Highlanders learned in school. The gentle courtesy was natural and had not had to be learned. "They stay at Mr. MacEwen's place. And there is the new fellow he has taken on to help him."

"A fellow? What kind of fellow would that be, now?"

"A black-haired lad with a canny enough mouth on him— or so my Elspeth said when she came back from bringing the milk. And with the looks on him like a prince, so she tells me, from a fairy tale—eyes blue as a harebell. A foolish eye it is some women have, sir."

"Thank you kindly," said the man with the eye-patch. He began to drop a coin into the Highlander's palm.

"No need for gold for a little common courtesy to a stranger, sir," said the Highlander with simple dignity, stepping back. ''Good night to you, sir. And I hope you find your lad.''

The man with the eye-patch caught up his horse and swung into the saddle. He rode away toward the Manse with the solid, easy seat of a professional soldier. And as the darkness closed about him, he loosened the pistols in his coat pocket.

Chapter 4

The Cock and Ninepins in Glasgow was filled with bustle and ablaze with light when Hal drove the cart into the inn yard. The stage had just come in. Fresh horses had already been run out and were being put to the shafts. He glanced around at the flaring torches and the scurrying grooms. And a problem of some import which had been nagging at him for the last two hours became charmingly clamorous in its immediacy. He had no money, no credit, and no influence. How the devil was he going to pay for a seat on the coach? Yet he was damned if he was going to allow Miss Prudence Drake to disappear on her mysterious errand alone. Did she really expect him to believe that she had no serious reason for creeping away from the Manse and fleeing south with a five-year-old boy?

Hal glanced back over his shoulder. The blond head of the child was snuggled into Prudence's plain brown coat. Dear Lord, but she wore damned ugly clothes! He would like to see her in a decent gown—he had a sudden vision of her in sheer ivory silk, her hair dressed with pearls to soften the severe bones of her face. It came to him with an odd sense of shock that such a thought seemed quite natural, as if he came from a world where ladies often wore ball gowns and no expense need be spared. But he had nothing to offer her, and God save him, as he studied her sleeping face, his real desire was to undress her. At which shameful thought, Hal saw Prudence sigh, open her eyes, and look about.

"Oh, heavens, we're here. Wake up, Bobby!"

The child clung sleepily to her arm as she attempted to extricate herself.

"Come, young man," said Hal, lifting the boy effortlessly into his arms. "We are going on a journey."

He slung Bobby onto his hip and walked into the office of the Cock and Ninepins. "I shall need three tickets on the Carlisle coach, sir," he said to the man behind the desk. "Inside seats, if you please."

The man looked up with distinct hostility at this cavalier request from a vagabond. "Inside's all bought up, my lad."

"Nevertheless, I have a young child here, as you see, and a lady. We shall require inside seats."

"That is," said Prudence behind him, "I require two seats inside. The gentleman may make separate arrangements."

"I am very sorry, ma'am," returned the man. "I have no inside seats at all. You should have purchased them ahead."

"Then would you have seats on the roof, sir?" asked Hal politely.

His voice carried a great deal of natural authority, but the man looked him up and down—at the reefer jacket, the scuffed trousers—and offered no humble obeisance at all.

"As it is, there is no room on the roof, either." Someone called and he got up and brushed past the little group. "You can stay here with your wife and bairn until tomorrow, of course. There are outside seats available tomorrow."

Prudence caught the man by the arm. "Pray, sir. Can you not make some accommodation, at least for myself and the child if this gentleman stays behind. I can pay in gold."

She began to take out her purse in order to show him, but Hal grasped her hand and forced it back into her pocket. "For God's sake, angel! Pray do not flash gold about in the public office!"

She shook herself free and looked pleadingly at the controller of tickets to Carlisle. But the man shook his head and gave her a genuine smile. "I'm sorry, lass. The flyer is all booked and loading now. Not even the king's crown would get you a seat this morning. And you should not be taking the bairn away from his father, now, should you? Especially when he wants to come."

And grinning at his own wit, he walked away.

Prudence sat down on a chair as Hal laughed down at her. "Wife and bairn?" he said. "Now, that has a lovely ring to it. Here, good wife, take our wee son for a moment, while I find you a way to get to England." Hal set Bobby down beside her, and Prudence pulled the child onto her lap.

"I don't think," she said as severely as she could, "that such a flagrant misunderstanding of our relationship is cause for levity!"

"But I would like it very much if Hal were my papa," said Bobby.

Then Prudence was amazed when Hal bent suddenly and took Bobby's small hand in his. "Alas, Bobby, circumstances do not allow such a thing to be. You do understand, don't you? But we can always be friends, even if we are far away from each other."

"Yes," replied Bobby quietly. "But faraway friends aren't much good when it's dark and little boys wake up in the night."

Prudence hugged the child to her. "You'll always have me," she said, and felt her heart tear as Bobby turned his face into her coat and wrapped his hands tightly around her neck.

Hal walked restlessly away for a moment, but then he turned and grinned at her again. "Do you really have a king's ransom in gold coin in your purse, angel?"

Pushing aside her worry and disappointment, Prudence nodded. She had no shortage of cash. But Lady Dunraven had announced that the public flyer was the fastest, safest way to get from Glasgow to England if she was discovered at the MacEwens'. Unless the pursuit was very hot on her trail, she would then be far from Scotland and in safety before Lord Belham's minions could begin to catch up. Now, instead, she was trapped like a pig in a poke at the Cock and Ninepins—with this mysterious rogue who couldn't resist teasing her!

The rogue was still grinning. "Then why don't I see if there is a private chaise for hire, with a driver. Would you want to pay for it if I can find one? Then the journey to England may be made in style."

"Mr. Hal," said Prudence, looking up at him. "I am grateful for your assistance, of course. But my funds are supplied by Bobby's grandmother. I don't think she would approve if I used them to pay for your expenses to England. I am very sorry, but that is how it is. I hope you will understand?"

"I understand and you misunderstand. I wouldn't dream of imposing on your employer's charity, angel."

"But I want Hal to come with us!" interjected Bobby.

Hal stooped down and met Bobby's eyes. "No, Miss Drake is right, sir. She is in honor bound to use your granny's blunt for you. I can't expect to come along unless I can pay my own way. There will be costs at every inn, and for fresh horses, and pay for the driver, and it would not sit very well with my honor, would it, if I did not provide a fair share of funds of my own? No gentleman would ever take such unconscionable advantage of a lady."

Bobby looked very earnestly into Hal's eyes, and slowly nodded. "But I would very much like you to come, all the same," he said quietly.

Hal reached out as if to brush his hand over the boy's shoulder, but instead he turned and walked away, leaving Prudence to face her confused thoughts. Of course she did not want him to come! But she had hardly expected that he would agree so easily, and she felt oddly and absurdly bereft. Nevertheless, it would never do to sit here in the coaching office like a ninny and fret about it, so after a moment she stood up with what she hoped was decision.

Taking Bobby by the hand Prudence led him into the warm inn parlor where she ordered hot chocolate and breakfast for them both. When Hal came back, she would at least insist on buying chocolate or coffee for him. Then she would ask him to convey the horse and cart back to Mr. MacEwen. Hal could stay on at the Manse, helping to test the new pistols and thus earning his keep, until he finally remembered who he was. And not for the first time, Prudence felt the most insistent stab of ignoble curiosity about that very question.

With a clatter of hooves and a blast of the horn, the over-loaded Carlisle Flyer left the yard. The bustle died away and the Cock and Ninepins became quiet. Prudence walked back and forth in the almost empty inn parlor, every once in a while peering from the window into the coach yard, while Bobby studied a series of risqué cartoons featuring the Prince Regent which were framed on the wall. Bobby had not yet learned to read script, so he could not decipher the scurrilous captions. The exaggerated drawings of the bulbous prince and his mistress were only amusing to a small child, so Prudence left him to it.

She watched idly as a man rode into the yard on a tall bay horse. The animal was lathered as if it had been pushed far too hard. Had the fellow ridden all night over the rough Highland tracks? Prudence hated inn yards for that very reason. The poor long-suffering horses that one saw there, sometimes exhausted or with sores visible under the harness, wrung her heart. It was a fact of everyday life, but Prudence felt she would never get used to it. Fortunately this horse did not seem to have been abused, he was only tired, and the rider gave him a pat as he swung to the ground and strode into the coaching office. But as the man passed under the torches, Prudence whirled back from the window as if burned. The rider had a long scar across one cheek, and above it his right eye was covered with an eye-patch.

The pursuit had already caught up!

She hurried over and whispered to Bobby. She had no clear idea what to do, but they couldn't sit here in the public parlor like rabbits in a trap!

"What, already fleeing again?" said an amused voice in her ear. Prudence spun about to look up into Hal's laughing face. "I have a chaise for you, dear Miss Drake. It awaits in the street and the driver is hired. The owner would like his payment, then you may be on your way."

Now that she knew for sure that Hal wasn't coming, Prudence felt the most inappropriate confusion of emotions. It was only civil to offer recognition for his services. But he was a complete stranger and a mystery. And it was essential to lose him, even if only because Hal seemed to have such a knack for disturbing her equilibrium. Nevertheless the production of the chaise seemed like a miracle. "Oh, gracious! This earns my undying gratitude, sir, truly! Thank you. Come on Bobby, Hal has found us a coach!"

They hurried out to the front of the inn, where a small light chaise and pair stood at the curb. A rotund gentleman with white side-whiskers beamed at her. "That's six guineas for the coach and three shillings for the driver, ma'am," he said after they had shaken hands and exchanged introductions.

Prudence rapidly counted out the coin as Hal organized the transfer of her luggage from the cart. Then she bundled Bobby into the chaise and began to climb in behind him. "Please ask the driver to start with all haste," she said to the white-whiskered gentleman. "I don't wish to lose a moment!" Now that the time had come she wasn't sure how to say good-bye to Hal, but the coach's owner did not realize that this was a sensitive moment.

"Och aye, ma'am, all's ready." The man turned to Hal and began to count out coins into his palm. "Here's your wages, sir, less my commission. Have a good journey and take care of my horses.''

Prudence put her head out of the window, and saw Hal spring up onto the box and take up the whip.

''Why, you double-dyed, insolent, unconscionable knave!''

His voice floated back down to her. ''What, Miss Drake, aren't you going to offer me congratulations? I have just secured honest employment so that I may hold up my head in society, and you accuse me of being a wastrel? Your driver, dear angel, is at your service.''

As the horses sprang forward Prudence pulled down the blind with a thud. How could he? But since the man with the eye-patch was already inside the Cock and Ninepins, there was no time to remonstrate. Let Hal drive her to Carlisle if he liked. Then she would lose him once and for all.

Dawn began to break. Prudence opened the shade, and she and Bobby looked back as Hal steadily drove the chaise up out of the fertile valley of the Clyde. Behind the sun-tipped spires of Glasgow rose the mountains of Argyleshire and the Campsie Fells. It was clear enough to see the peak of Ben Lomond, washed with pink and primrose. A lump rose in her throat. She was about to pass through the country of her childhood, and she had never left Scotland before.

It took more than three hours to reach Lanark. Their only stops would be to change horses, and Hal had been driving steadily, accurately, and fast, but the road took precipitous turns through the craggy country. While the horses were being changed Prudence bought a large basket of provisions at the inn, and Hal indulged himself with venison pie and a bottle of wine. Then Bobby sat up on the box with Hal as he drove up across the bleak, treeless tops of the Southern Uplands, past Crawford and the gold and lead-rich Elvan Water, the great peak of Lowther Law rising ahead. Water seemed to run and sparkle everywhere, for these open wastes were the headwaters of both the Clyde and the Nith.

At last they left the straggle of heather-thatched mining villages behind and trotted on past Ballencleuch Law, looming threateningly to the left as a shadow cast by the high floating clouds darkened the peak for a moment. Prudence leaned back against the squabs and felt a rush of fear. What had she undertaken to do? When she had promised old Lady Dunraven to take Bobby away into hiding, she had never thought for one moment that deadly pursuit might be so close on her trail. The sun blazed out once again, throwing a shaft of golden light across her skirts. Prudence felt the carriage rock as Hal suddenly pulled up the horses, leapt down, and came to the window.

"Below us, if the directions of our kind chaise-owner are correct, is Nithsdale, ma'am, and it's all downhill from here," he said. "Shall we have a picnic dinner?"

Prudence thought of that long scar running down below an eye-patch. "Must we stop? Pray, I wish we might hurry!"

"Good God, angel, we are hurrying. It is usual, I understand, to make Glasgow to Carlisle a two-day journey. I need a break. We shall still be in Carlisle well before midnight. Isn't that good enough?"

Prudence colored. Hal had been driving for over nine hours, counting the time in the pony cart. It would take another seven or eight hours at least to reach Carlisle. And there were several roads south out of Glasgow. Even if the man with the eye-patch had discovered that a woman with a blond boy had been trying to get a seat on the Carlisle coach, he could not know which way they had gone. And hopefully, his inquiries would have taken some time. The innkeeper hadn't seemed the type to easily volunteer much information.

She peered from the window and found without surprise that she was already close to exhaustion herself. And then she saw why Hal had stopped in this particular spot. There was a scattering of huge granite boulders at a turn of the road. Several trees were growing in their beneficent shelter; it was a perfect spot to bait the horses and sit in the sun for a picnic. For below them stretched a valley and—magically claiming her attention—at the mouth of a narrow gorge towered an ancient castle, isolated and ruined. Water ran leaping and foaming in a waterfall around its rocky feet, throwing spume high against the moss-covered walls. Trees clustered thickly, some having taken root in the walls of the gorge itself, so that the castle seemed almost to float as if it were unreal—a mirage that might disappear at any moment.

"It seemed," said Hal with his light humor as he examined the scene, "that this was a particularly romantic and picturesque spot, which deserved our admiration, if not our rapturous breaking into verse. But, alas, the only poetry to which I could bend my wanton tongue would be most unsuitable for the scene below us, don't you think?"

So Prudence found herself climbing from the carriage, wishing that she might be anywhere but here—with this uncertain rogue, on a treacherously lovely day, in a heart-breakingly beautiful place. Bobby raced about on the grass, laughing and skipping, while Hal took the basket from the chaise and unwrapped his own provisions which he had tied up in a square of cloth. He spread a blanket from the carriage and invited Prudence to sit. Then, far from displaying the retiring habits of a servant, Hal dropped down beside her. He shrugged out of his jacket and used it to make a cushion for her back. Then he leaned his shoulders against the sloping wall of granite and stretched out his lean, strong legs, his booted feet negligently crossed at the ankle, so that Prudence was painfully aware of the graceful lines of his body. Bobby curled up beside Hal. They of course shared their food. It was a perfect, marvelous picnic that left Prudence devastated.

For as they feasted on the fresh bread and fruit, the cold meats and cheeses, Hal began to tell Bobby a story. He wove into the tale every element of high romance that could be imagined, and then took the story into flights of wonder. The ruined castle became populated before her eyes with stalwart, long-haired warriors, armor shining; lovely princesses, sad with longing; scaly dragons breathing fire; swart hobgoblins, trolls, and giants; and wild swans keening their wild cries overhead. Forests became enchanted; trees had voices; and flowers sprang where maidens put their feet. When Hal finished, Bobby— every sense filled and satisfied, eyes shining with happiness— fell asleep against the story-teller's knee. Hal gently picked the child up and carried him to the chaise.

Prudence stood and leaned against the great outcropping of granite that had sheltered them. She closed her eyes and let the warm afternoon sunshine beat down on her lids. For no reason she could fathom, she felt tears pricking and a painful lump in her throat. She knew herself emotionally lost, searching for some thread to hold her to the earth—she felt voiceless, humbled, entranced. A light touch brushed across her hair, and a hand was gently but firmly laid over her closed lids.

"No," said Hal's voice. "Don't open your eyes."

Prudence trembled as she stood there, blinded by his fingers, her senses alert to him: his clean scent mingled faintly with that of leather and horses; the knowledge that he towered over her, slim and lean; the clear memory of his features; the soft, regular rhythm of his breath.

"For only a moment, angel," he whispered into her ear. "For one moment out of time, relax into the zenith. This is the enthralling land of Faerie. No rules apply here."

His hand moved, but Prudence was filled with a disturbing longing. She left her eyes closed to block her tears. A small tremor swayed her as she felt him pull the pins from her hair. It fell lightly around her neck and across her shoulders. Then she could feel it being smoothed back, until his long, firm fingers slipped behind her head. But Prudence did not dare to look into that long-lashed harebell gaze. So to her shame, like the princess of the fairy tale, she stood enchanted as Hal touched her shaking lips with his own and began to tease nectar from her mouth.

Ah, the delicate, wild, insistent taste of his lips! And all the while he was stroking her hair in long, sensuous waves down her back.

"Your hair is shining in the sun like the magic strands of silk which bound the jester to his lute," he murmured against her mouth. "With your hair down, you are someone else. Be that person while you may, angel. 'Let us go, while we are in our prime / And take the harmless folly of the time!' You may be as angry with me as you like afterwards. After all, when we get to Carlisle, I won't be employed any longer, will I?"

His touch was gone. Prudence opened her eyes to see him striding away to disappear behind the boulder. She sank to the ground and squatted there for a moment with her hand over her mouth. Oh, dear Lord! She was nothing better than a hussy. She hadn't objected, or pushed him away, or closed her mouth. Miss Prudence Drake had stood there like a ninny, seduced by a fairy tale, and had her senses sweetly ravished. She forced herself to stand and squaring her shoulders pulled replacement pins out of her pocket. Rapidly she put up her hair.

The carriage horses looked softly at her over their nose-bags as Prudence climbed back into the chaise next to the sleeping child. A few moments later, she heard Hal untie the horses, put the feed-bags away, and climb onto the box. In the next hour they had dropped down into the valley and passed through the long village of Thornhill. They would reach Dumfries in two hours. Then by the time they came into Annan it would be dark. And before midnight they would reach Carlisle, where there would be innumerable coaches to England, and she could say good-bye to Hal forever. Prudence felt the force of that future with a strange desolation, as tears slipped silently down her cheeks.

Prudence awoke to a confusion of shouts and curses. The chaise had lurched to a sudden halt, and Bobby startled beside her and cried out. She heard the sound of Hal's voice, soothing, yet authoritative, and the voices of several men and a woman, screaming and wailing. Then Hal came to the door and looked in.

"I am very sorry, Miss Drake," he said formally. "There has been a small accident. No one is hurt, but the road is blocked. We may have to stop here for some time."

She rubbed the sleep from her eyes. "Where are we?"

Hal turned away for a moment and made inquiries. "Two hours from our destination," he said after a moment. "We lack but fourteen miles or so to Carlisle. Longtown and romantic Lochinvar are lost in the murky dark ahead of us. And we are stranded at Graitney."

Prudence peered from the coach window, her arm around Bobby who stared wide-eyed into the night. They seemed to be in the main street of a small village. Beyond a straggle of houses the countryside stretched away into a flat, barren darkness. Several men ran up with torches. The road was blocked by a large wagon which was entangled with an overturned carriage. The occupants, a young girl and a man at least ten years her senior, were standing in the road arguing.

"I shan't marry you at all!" the girl cried. "Look what you have done! You've run us into a great hay wain, dumped me into the road, and spoiled my pelisse."

"By God, Sarah," returned the man. "If all you can mind is your damned pelisse, I'll be glad to let you go home to your father without a wedding, and that's the Lord's own truth!"

The girl began to wail in great wrenching sobs.

"I believe," said Hal with a swallowed smile. "That we are witnessing the ruins of an elopement. I am given to understand that it is less than a mile to the border. But whatever we may think about the young lady's dashed hopes, her swain has crashed his carriage against that large wagon and we cannot pass. Shall we go into the inn and refresh ourselves while we await developments?"

Prudence took Bobby by the hand and climbed from the chaise. A boy ran out from the inn and took charge of their carriage. She allowed Hal to give her his arm and they walked together into Graitney Hall, the only inn in the place.

"Here comes the couple, Mr. Scott!" cried someone as Hal pushed open the door and they stepped inside.

"Ah, the poor tired bairn!" said a plump woman in an apron. "He'd like some warm milk in the kitchen, I'll be bound."

Bobby was snatched away and carried triumphantly off in the woman's arms.

A rotund man with a smile like a hay rake beamed at Hal and Prudence. He seemed to be very splendidly foxed, and most likely the proprietor.

"Bless you, my dears!" he cried. "What might your names be now?"

"This is Miss Prudence Drake," said Hal. "She will require a private room for herself and the child until the road to England is cleared. I am Hal, her driver."

"Then before these witnesses and almighty God, I declare you, Mr. Hal Herdriver, and you, Miss Prudence Drake, man and wife and bound together in holy matrimony from this day forth. That'll be a shilling. Write up the paper, Jimmy! Go on, lad, kiss your bride!"

And as Prudence opened her mouth to object, Hal couldn't restrain himself. Glazed with exhaustion, but luminous with laughter, he leant down and kissed Prudence with a thoroughness that was obviously entirely unnecessary. Warmth and sweet moisture invaded her senses again, leaving her weak at the knees, the blood hammering in her veins. It was so unfair! How could he?

"There you are, my dears," said the rotund man. "Here are your marriage lines!"

"This is nonsense!" announced Prudence as soon as Hal released her. "We aren't here to be married!"

"Man and wife, right and tight!" the man replied. "And for the sake of giving the wee lad a name, forget the shilling! I've had enough damned ale for one night!'' And thrusting a dirty piece of paper at Hal, the rotund gentleman slumped to the floor.

Hal burst out laughing and slipped the paper into his pocket, while Prudence stalked away, pushing through the crowd after Bobby. She found him happily drinking warm milk in the kitchen.

''Hello, Miss Drake,'' he said. ''This is a very nice place, I think.''

''A famous enough place and that's a fact!'' exclaimed the plump woman. ''All the English lads and lasses run away to marry in Graitney—Gretna Green, they call it, though some can't wait so long and marry right there in the toll booth on the high road, a half mile before they get here!''

''I did not come here to be married!'' said Prudence quietly. ''I would like somewhere private for myself and the child, please.''

The woman showed her to a bedchamber upstairs, and invited her to lie down while the road was being cleared, but Prudence could not relax. The absurd marriage she instantly dismissed. It was obviously not legal—there was no Mr. Herdriver, after all! But who was he? Hal had entranced her so simply, so easily, and not only by assailing her body—though there was that too in the end—but by enthralling her mind. Was he a rake? Did he make a practice of carelessly seducing women? And why her? A plain, straight laced governess!

She was pacing back and forth while Bobby looked at a book by the light of a candle, when a sudden tumult of noise from the courtyard below brought them both to the window.

A crowd had poured out of the inn. A huge ox of a man strode at their head, roaring out threats to the night sky. There was a great deal of shouting and gesticulating. Almost everyone seemed to be drunk. Half-carried by the mob, then hoisted shoulder high for a moment, was a dark-haired man. The crowd formed a circle and dropped him into its center. As his coat, then his shirt, were dragged off by a multitude of hands, leaving his lithe body naked to the night air from the waist up, the young man's only response seemed to be helpless laughter.

"What is happening, Miss Drake?" cried Bobby, clutching her hand. "What are they going to do to Hal?"

Chapter 5

Hal had let Prudence follow after Bobby without interference. Then he surveyed the public bar and weighed up his chances of mending his fortunes. If he was to follow Miss Drake past Carlisle, he must parlay his few shillings into guineas. He had no idea what skills he might possess which would enable him to do so. He could shoot, of course, but he had no pistol and there was no one in this motley crowd who seemed likely to want to wager on a shooting match. Perhaps he had skill at dice or cards, but he couldn't risk his small purse while he found out. And in the meantime it seemed that the only thing about to be tested was his head for hard liquor, for every man there seemed eager to buy him a drink. Hal tossed back innumerable toasts, knowing that he would soon be forced to pay for their treat in turn. Was nothing to come out of this but a sore head and depleted pockets? He reluctantly downed another potent glass.

"And here is the truth of it, then," one of the drunks was saying to the crowd. "That yon Sassenach are nae match for a Scots fighting man! It's aye the Scots at the front of every battle!''

"There's ne'er a lad south of the border can match ye, Jamie!'' replied another soothingly. "Ye are the very de'il of a man in a fight and we all ken it fine.''

"Then wha'll fight me the night?'' insisted Jamie, his red-rimmed eyes sweeping the room. "O' all yon English loons.'' He waved a fist with the stubby forefinger pointing in menace, indicating several of the Englishmen there. "Wha'll put up his fives, eh?''

"Yon English are all lubberly cowards and we all ken it. It is a braw, bonny, fine figure of fighter ye are, lad. There's nae Sassenach could stand one round against ye, Jamie.''

"And would you wager your blunt on that, sir?'' said someone in a cultured London accent. "I'll give a purse of two guineas to any Englishman here that proves you wrong.''

Hal glanced at the speaker: a tall fellow with brown hair and a nose like a beak. His clothes spoke of wealth; his voice of an idle, cultivated boredom, ready for anything which would act as an entertaining distraction from the routines of life. As the crowd cheered, the gentleman pulled out a purse and counted out the prize money.

"Who will stand up for the honor of his country?'' he asked casually, and his brown eye rested speculatively for a moment on Hal.

"What a perfect, apposite, and absurd end to a splendid day. I'd be happy to take the challenge,'' Hal heard himself say in what seemed to be an inebriated show of bravado. "But for five guineas and a bonus if I level Mr. James in one blow.''

There was instantly an uproar of speculation. "I'll wager ye twa shillings that yon sleekit Englishman will nae stand up to one round with Braw Jamie!''

So as the betting books filled, Hal found himself manhandled out into the courtyard, where under the flare of the flambeaux Jamie was stripping off his coat and shirt. The man was muscled like an ox. Hal heard a faint echo of his own voice saying: *I feel as if I just took the worst from the knuckles of Gentleman Jackson.* He had no idea if that had been just an idle boast, or if he did indeed know how to box. And even if he did, would the half-drunk Jamie follow the gentleman's code, or just start swinging like a savage? Of course, Hal wasn't quite as clear-headed himself as he would like to have been, which added a certain piquancy to the event.

The mob divested him of his coat and shirt, and the cold night air washed over his back and chest like a rush of snow melt running off a mountain. Feeling instantly more sober, Hal rapidly wrapped his knuckles in strips of cloth provided by the plump woman, and assessed his chances. He had been driving all day. His shoulders and arms were still burning with the strain of it. The warm glow of whisky in his belly was wantonly weighing down his reactions. Hal glanced up at his opponent, who was flexing gigantic muscles to the admiration of the crowd, and tried without success to suppress an upwelling of laughter. It wasn't going to do Prudence any good at all if he was beaten to a pulp before he even had her out of Scotland!

An anticipatory hush fell over the crowd. There was nothing but the sound of Jamie's heavy panting and his own quick breath, hard and sharp in Hal's ears. But he stepped forward and shook Jamie by his great paw of a hand. The man returned it in a grip designed to break every bone.

"Nae blows below the belt," said one of the Scotsmen who seemed to have taken on the role of referee. "Nae kicks wi' the feet, nor hidden weapons. Have at it, then, lads!"

The two men circled each other for a moment, then Jamie came in swinging his great hands like steam hammers.

Prudence watched from the room above, transfixed. "Oh, dear Lord," she breathed. "That man will kill him!"

"No, he won't," said Bobby. "Hal's home is the sea and he's the strongest man there is."

Prudence hugged the child to her. She ought to forbid him

to watch! For Hal was obviously not the stronger. He was lean and hard, but lightly built, though mitered muscles ran clearly defined on his back and shoulders. His opponent outweighed him by at least three stone. Jamie had huge slabs of brawn across his chest, and arms built like tree limbs. Prudence flinched as a mammoth fist swung at the laughing face under the black hair, threatening to smash the fine bones into splinters. Yet Hal seemed perfectly relaxed. Without visible effort he ducked away from the blow, then almost casually landed one of his own against the side of the giant's head. The crowd roared.

Ah, so he did know how to box, after all! Hal danced and spun, ducking and blocking as Jamie came flailing into the attack.

"Come, Jamie," he said between breaths. "Take another stab, man. I might be annihilated just by the sheer wind of it as it goes past my ear."

Several heavy blows rained about his head. Hal swirled away from the worst of them, but one great fist caught him hard in the shoulder. For too long his entire right arm was numb to the wrist, but he managed to raise it just enough to block the next incoming attack. With his left he landed another blow of his own and Jamie staggered back with a look of open, comic surprise on his red face.

" 'He stayed not for brake, and he stopped not for stone, / He swam the Eske river where ford there was none,' " gasped Hal. " 'For a laggard in love, and a dastard in war, / Was to wed the fair Ellen of brave Lochinvar.' "

It seemed appropriate only because the River Eske lay so close. But Jamie seemed to think the verses an insult. He roared like a lion and enthusiastically swung back into the mill.

" 'Love swells like the Solway, but ebbs like its tide,' " added Hal. " 'So faithful in love, and so dauntless in war, / There never was knight like the young Lochinvar.' "

And then Hal had no more breath left for poetry.

For although Jamie was very drunk—more foxed than Hal was, and making more mistakes—the man was a vicious fighter. Hal managed to land several more blows to the man's chin and chest. But his punches would never knock down this monster, and simple, unforgiving fatigue was taking its toll. Hal's shoulders had begun a fierce burn, and every reaction came more slowly. He began to fall back, the crowd surging away behind him, as Jamie came in for the final annihilation. The blows came too quickly now to dodge them all.

" 'And save his good broadsword, he weapon had none,' " gasped Hal, as a fist skimmed past his ear, grazing his cheek, but another landed square in his belly, forcing the air from his lungs in a sickening rush.

Then he began to fight for his life.

Prudence hated it. She hated the sense of stupid, animal ferocity, and the dark bruises blossoming like evil flowers on the men's bodies. She hated the rapacious faces of the crowd, wagering their money on other men's pain. Yet against her will she was enthralled. Fascinated by the grace of Hal's movements, and his cavalier, laughing disregard for the fact that sooner or later the big man would beat him down and destroy him. Fascinated by the strange beauty of a man's body, flexing and twisting in deadly combat. Fascinated by Hal's wide, hard-ridged shoulders and strong, slim waist, dancing in the torch light.

And then before she could quite fathom that it was over, she saw Jamie begin to fall. Hal spun out of his way as the man dropped to his knees. Jamie swung his head back and forth for a moment, like a bull blinded by dust, then thudded to the ground. The onlookers surged forward, but the giant lay staring vacantly up at the sky. Hal's voice floated up to her above the roar of the crowd, ragged with his disordered breathing, but still clear and deadly.

"Alas!" he said. "What sport is this? 'She is won! we are

gone! over bank, bush, and scaur; / They'll have fleet steeds that follow, quoth young Lochinvar.' "

And then laughing and glazed with exhaustion, he allowed the gentleman with the beaked nose to wrap his shirt around his shoulders and press something into his hand.

Prudence pulled Bobby from the window and sat with him on the bed for several long minutes as she stared out at the night sky.

She felt like weeping and yet she was very angry. Damnation to the beautiful, mysterious Hal!

"You see," said Bobby. "I said Hal was the stronger. And now will he drive us to Carlisle?"

"With pleasure," said a voice from the doorway. "I am led to believe that the road is now clear. Our nags are rested. We can arrive in Carlisle before tomorrow yet."

"Are you mad?" Prudence whirled around. "What on earth was that about?"

"No, no, angel," replied Hal, coming into the room. "I have taken enough blows already. Pray do not add to them!"

He had obviously sluiced himself with water. The black hair was damp and ruffled as if rapidly dried in a towel. A great rent had appeared in one seam of his jacket. He looked like a gypsy—wild and untamed. Bobby ran up to him. Without visibly wincing, Hal swung the child up into his arms.

Prudence stood and faced him. She was shaking. "You must be a wastrel! Or a lunatic! Or a scoundrel!"

"I have wondered as much," said Hal seriously. A black bruise was beginning to color his cheek. "I have no idea, of course. I might be just a man-about-town, who fills his idle hours with pugilism." Then he looked straight into her eyes, and Prudence saw how carefully his emotions were guarded, emotions that he covered with flippancy and with sarcasm. "And earlier it seemed as if I must be a rake, didn't it? Of course, both boxing and flirtation are pursuits of the idle Corinthian as much as of the rogue. So I still might be just a respectable man with a competence."

"No respectable man would take up a challenge to indulge in drunken fisticuffs. It would go against every instinct!"

"Then I am a disreputable fellow, after all? For of course no respectable man would treat a lady as I have treated you, stealing kisses as if they were his due. Do you think I'm a Don Juan and a profligate?"

"I think it very likely," snapped Prudence.

Hal dropped to a chair and leaned his head back. "A challenge?" he asked with a grin. "It seems to me that there is only one way to find out, isn't there? You must help me discover, Miss Drake, how much of a rake I am. In the meantime, I intend to take you to Carlisle, as promised. For whatever I am—and the delightful state of not knowing is proving most soothing to my soul, I must say—I intend to keep my word."

Prudence blushed, just a little. "You cannot mean to drive me to Carlisle after this," she said.

"Why not? I am paid and contracted to do so. Come, Bobby, let us return to our carriage."

She resented it, but she followed him down the stairs and out into the night. Their carriage was waiting.

The famous Eske river was crossed by a bridge. Less than two hours later, they arrived at Carlisle. The George Inn was jammed with passengers just arriving from the south. Prudence pushed through the crowd, and booked and paid for tickets on the mail coach the next day as far as Liverpool. Then she secured a room for herself and Bobby for the night. But before she could either thank him or admonish him again, Hal had disappeared.

In spite of his burning fatigue, Hal could not sleep. He shared a room in the attic with two other travelers whose snores rumbled into the quiet night. Why the devil had he kissed Prudence Drake? To find out if he was indeed a rake? *She had trembled in his hands like a doe!* It had been strangely delightful, but if he was setting himself up as her knight errant, he hadn't exactly made a very good start. But where was she going in such haste? And why did fear travel with her? Finally, lulled by his companion's snores, Hal drifted into the sleep of deep exhaustion.

He dreamt. There was the voice of a woman. Her words seemed faint and remote. She was arguing with someone: *"But he broke into the house!"*

Hal heard someone saying her name, someone who meant everything to him—a man he would give his life for, if it was asked. "Helena. Go to bed, Helena."

And Helena was gazing down at him, her features full of fear and anger, and her blond hair brightly haloed by candlelight. As he looked up at her, the lovely face wavered and changed, and it was Prudence Drake who stood over him. The expression of distaste on her severe features threatened to break his heart. "Smile for me, sweet angel," he heard himself say. But she turned away from him in disgust.

When he awoke, the other men were gone. Hal dragged himself out of the bed. He shrugged into his shirt and winced as his sore muscles made protest. Yet at least the pugnacious Jamie had broken no bones. His face looked back at him from the small mirror over the dresser, and he surveyed it without pleasure. He was lucky not to have a black eye, for one cheek was marked with a magnificent bruise.

And then as if his dreams continued, he heard his own voice, *"How the hell is the family's name for elegance to be kept up if you will keep appearing in public brindled like a cow?"*

Hal went close to the mirror and pushed his untidy hair back from his forehead. He studied the blue eyes and the high cheekbones. So he had a family with a name for elegance? All he vaguely remembered were the names of some children. Who were they? Who was he? Were there men and women out there somewhere who looked like him? Who missed him? Did anyone care that he had disappeared? And who the devil was Helena? Then he laughed at himself. Perhaps if he had let Jamie beat him to a pulp, he would have remembered. Isn't that what usually happened with head injuries in novels?—one did the damage, but a second repaired it.

Hal slung on his torn jacket and went downstairs to pick up the horse he had arranged to rent for ten shillings the night before. It was past eight. The Liverpool coach had already left—a discovery he made without asking, because someone else was making the inquiries for him. From instinct Hal drew back and concealed himself behind a pillar as he heard a man's voice, "I've been asking at every inn in town, sir. I'm looking for a black-haired fellow traveling south with a woman and a little boy. The lad's blond and bright for his age. The man is youngish, tall and good-looking, has an air about him; you'd not miss him."

"The coach south has gone, sir," said the innkeeper, "these three hours since. And there was no party on it that matches your description, although there were four children among the passengers, and one was a blond lad, right enough."

As the man turned away and walked out into the streets of Carlisle, Hal knew he would be easy enough to recognize again. The poor fellow had a scar down the length of his cheek and wore a black patch over one eye.

Bobby did not weep or throw a tantrum when he realized that they were leaving without Hal, but his stoic silence almost broke Prudence's heart. They had left Carlisle at five that morning and had breakfast in Penrith. Then she stared dully out of the window as the coach climbed up over the heath and across Shap Fells. The famous peaks of the Lake District spread out to her right. Once she had dreamed of being able to wander, "lonely as a cloud," through those famous hills and valleys. Now the coach sped past them, while one of the passengers rattled off the names and quoted long passages from Wordsworth. Although they were some of her favorite poems, Prudence hardly heard them, for her mind was filled with images of Hal. She had let him kiss her—twice! A man who would strip himself to the waist and fight like a beast for a purse full of guineas. She didn't know who she despised most: Hal or herself. *But she had left him behind. She had left him behind!*

After a steep descent into Kendal, the coach began to travel through fertile valleys filled with fields and trees. Burton, Lancaster, Preston, Ormskirk, passed in a blur, until at last just before ten o'clock that night they arrived in the coach yard of the Royal Oak in Liverpool, and Prudence discovered that she had no money.

She frantically turned out all of her pockets and her little collection of luggage, while Bobby helped by keeping up a running commentary on all the extraordinary things he had seen from the coach.

"That lady said those big standing stones we saw past Shap were a Druidical Relique, Miss Drake," Bobby said earnestly. "What is that? Who were the Druids? And why does the rock change color? It was gray on the fells, and then black, and then red. Why is that? What did that man mean by saying that hill was Arthur's Round Table? It didn't look like a table, did it?"

"Hush, Bobby. I am busy." All she found were a few shillings in the pocket of her pelisse. The purse of gold was gone. Dear God, help her! She had carried Lady Dunraven's coins tied securely at her belt. It had been a comforting weight. How could she not have instantly missed it? When had it disappeared? Prudence sat down on her bag and hugged Bobby to her side. There was no answer. But somewhere, at one of the inns, at Penrith or at Shap or at Lancaster, or even last night at Carlisle after she had paid for her room and passage, someone had stolen her money and she hadn't even noticed. Oh, dear Lord, what was she going to do now?

"Come, now, ma'am," said the innkeeper's voice. "Did you want a room or not?"

"Might I ask for a room on credit, sir?" she asked. "I believe I have been robbed."

Within three minutes, she and Bobby were standing together on the streets of a strange city, their luggage tossed out behind them, while the dark mist of a Liverpool night wreathed about through the houses. As if to add color to her plight, it began to rain. Prudence reached into one of her bags and pulled out her umbrella.

"I think, sir," she said to Bobby. "That we had better find some other kind of shelter."

"What, angel? Is the Royal Oak not to your taste?"

"Hal!" squealed Bobby. Prudence lifted her umbrella and saw him standing there, smiling at her. The child launched himself into Hal's arms. "Hal, we have been robbed and the nasty man at the inn won't let us stay, and Miss Drake and I have nowhere to go."

"You've been robbed?" asked Hal, sharply. "Where? When?"

"I don't know," said Prudence. "But I have only a few shillings left to my name."

"Then thank goodness I won my guineas last night, angel. Come, we'll at least buy dinner—but not at the Royal Oak, alas. We shall have to conserve our small purse, won't we?"

Hal shouldered the luggage and strode away down the street, Prudence and Bobby at his heels. Within a few minutes they were inside the dining room of a small, plain hostelry. Bobby ate a large bowl of soup while Hal maintained a light, flippant conversation about hired horses. Finally the child fell asleep against Prudence's lap. Then Hal leaned back and the harebell eyes narrowed between the black lashes as he looked at Prudence.

"Very well," he said. "I want to know what the devil is going on. I happened to overhear your pursuer asking after you at Carlisle. Why are you fleeing into England with the young Earl of Dunraven? And why are you being followed by a man with an eye-patch?"

Her confused rush of anger and, oddly, relief that Hal knew of her predicament left Prudence breathless for a moment. "How do you know about Bobby?"

"My dear Miss Drake, Bobby told me his name and that he

was a lord back at the Manse. A few very discreet inquiries
gave me the details. Henry, the last earl, died in London recently
and Bobby is now the fifth Lord Dunraven—small owner of
his own vast estates and a castle. Yet you are flying in terror
from Scotland and you are being followed. I want to know
why.''

So Prudence told him: about Lord Belham, about the guardianship, about the threat to Bobby's life.

''And where are you taking him?''

''To my sister in Wiltshire. Her husband's a magistrate.
Bobby will be safe there.''

Hal stared at her, and then he put his head in his hands to
hide his reaction—which was close to hilarity. ''Oh, Lord!
This is insanity, angel! The whole thing is preposterous! A
piece of absolutely perfect folly! You mean to tell me that
Lady Dunraven sends her vulnerable little grandson away into
England with no protection but his charming, innocent governess—who has never been out of Scotland before—because
they are being sought by a lethal marquess?''

Prudence bridled. ''I don't care how foolish it seems. That
is what happened.''

''So now you land in Liverpool, robbed of your purse, and
with the pursuit hot on your trail. I think, my dear, that I shall
have to rescue you.''

''How do I know that I can trust you?'' asked Prudence in
a small voice. ''What payment would you want?''

Hal stood up and walked back and forth for a moment. Then
he came back and sat down again opposite her. ''You cannot
know that you can trust me, Miss Drake. How can I know
whether I can trust myself, when I don't know who I am? We
shall both have to gamble on that. Yet I will undertake to get
you and Bobby to your sister, and we shall throw the man with
the eye-patch off our trail.''

''And the payment?''

He grinned playfully. ''To put up with my company, of
course. The company of a fellow who is probably a rake and

a wastrel, and who certainly intends to find out." He winked
at her. "I might take my payment in kisses, I think. Nevertheless, with your few shillings, you don't have much choice, do
you? And I shall protect you with my last breath from the
fellow with the eye-patch."

Although she knew he was teasing her, Prudence bridled.
"At least I know that you can knock down a man twice your
size!"

"You refer to the elegant Jamie? Alas, angel, I did not knock
him down. When the drink finally seized his befuddled brain,
he fell like a tree of his own accord. Had he not been foxed,
I assure you that you might have left a wreath on my grave in
Gretna Green. I hope you would have purchased a large and
grand one, full of lilac—for youthful innocence, broken engage-
ments, and sad death. 'O were my Love yon lilac fair'!"

Which surprised Prudence into laughter. "Very well, sir, for
Bobby's sake, pray rescue us. You have a plan?"

"Alas, I have several. And I think we had better put the first
one into operation right now. How much of that luggage is
really necessary?"

"Most of it."

"Really necessary!"

"I could leave one bag, perhaps, if it was all repacked."

"Good, then do it."

So Prudence repacked the things she had brought for herself
and Bobby, so that one bag could be left behind. Hal arranged
that it be sent to Lady Dunraven, charges to be paid upon
arrival. He then took Prudence and Bobby away from the main
streets and into a poorer, though still moderately respectable,
part of town where he secured a room for the night for Mr.
and Mrs. Herdriver and child.

"Do not remonstrate, Miss Drake," he whispered in her ear
as she overheard him make this arrangement with the landlady.
"But from now on we shall travel as man and wife. Otherwise
our situation will cause comment and we shall be remembered

and refused service. Don't worry, our friend with the eye-patch will not find us here.''

They were shown into an attic room with one large bed. Hal dumped the bags in the corner and helped Prudence pull the clothes from the sleepy child. Soon Bobby was in his little nightshirt and tucked into the center of the bed.

''Now we too shall repair to innocent slumber, angel. I hope there are no fleas,'' said Hal, and he blew out the candle.

Prudence was painfully aware of every sound in the dark room. She wondered for a moment if she should go to bed fully clothed. But it seemed a most unpleasant sacrifice to modesty, so she tried to slide off her dress without noise. To her chagrin it seemed to rustle in the most suggestive way. Meanwhile she heard Hal's jacket hit the chair and his boots thump to the floor. She sat on the edge of the bed and unlaced her traveling boots, then debated whether she should remove her stockings. It was beyond all bounds of propriety to be here, sharing a room with a man, even if Bobby was a perfect chaperon, but somehow to have naked feet and legs made it all the worse. Yet she never slept in her stockings! So finally she unrolled them, rinsed them at the washstand, and set them neatly to dry above the dresser beside her clothes. She heard Hal pull off his shirt and toss it after his jacket. In the darkness it glimmered a little, like a ghost. Keeping her back to the dark, masculine shape, now stripping off his trousers, Prudence slipped her capacious nightdress over her head and within its reassuring shelter wriggled out of her shift. Hal was already between the sheets. Prudence stood in the dark room and looked at the bed. The most uncomfortable feelings seemed to be spreading through her blood. She had nothing to protect her from ruin but her night rail, and her innocent faith in the dampening presence of a five-year-old boy.

Chapter 6

When she awoke, Hal had gone. The steady breath next to her was only Bobby's. Prudence scrambled out of the bed and into her clothes before Hal could return. She was, thanks to her foolish inability to protect her own purse, entirely in the hands of the mysterious stranger from the beach. It already seemed a lifetime ago that she had found him there, washed up like drift wood. He came back to the room with pork pies for breakfast, and news that the man with the eye-patch had scoured every coaching inn and was watching the main road south to London. It was still barely light.

"Our friend has been liberal with bribes and encouragement to the ostlers. We should not be able to take horses from any inn in town and not have him after us within the hour," he finished.

"But you have a plan," said Bobby. "And we shall be safe."

Prudence had informed the child that they were hiding from someone who was after them. She had not told him why, or that it was serious. For Bobby, the journey was still just a grand game.

"Come," said Hal. "And you'll see. I have found a man with a boat."

They did not take the regular passenger ferry across the Mersey to Birkenhead. Instead a disreputable-looking fellow in a flat cap rowed them in his little boat up the wide pool of the estuary and into the mouth of the River Weaver. He finally put them ashore near a cluster of warehouses and docks on the south side of Runcorn.

"Here you are, then, sir," he said.

Hal counted out some coins and grinned at Prudence as the man speedily turned his boat and disappeared into the early morning mist.

"Who on earth was that?"

"Very probably a smuggler," replied Hal. "And his fees have already dangerously depleted my slim purse. So from here, angel, I shall work our passage. Would you prefer to travel with coal, salt, limestone, or clay?"

Half an hour later Prudence discovered the plan. Hal secured work and a sleeping nook for them both on a narrow boat which was about to set out down the Grand Trunk Canal for the potteries of Stoke-on-Trent. The name of the boat was painted in bright colors at her bow: *The White Lady*. The boatman, whose name—Sam Masters—marched across the panels of the tiny cabin amid a revel of blue and red flowers, was willing to take on an extra hand in trade for board and passage, but he wasn't too sure about the woman and boy.

"She's not the mother of that lad," Sam Masters said suspiciously. "She's not old enough."

"Oh, the boy's mine, from a previous liaison," replied Hal with a wink. "But the lady is my wife."

The man looked them both up and down. "I'm a widower with just the one son to help me, but I'm not a fool, sir. We're godly folk. I'll not take your strumpet along."

"Good heavens, the lady and I are legally married. And here's the paper to prove it." Hal pulled out the marriage lines that they had been given in Gretna Green.

"Then you are newly-weds!" The boatman's face creased into sudden smiles. "Canal folk often travel with their wives, sir, and I don't blame you for wanting to bring your bride along. The little lad can sleep with my Willie, and I'll find a private spot for you and the lassie, shall I?"

"My lord."

The footman bowed low over the silver tray which he held out to the marquess. It was the trained, ingratiating manner of the very best London servant, which irritated Lord Belham enough to make him frown darkly at the man and send him scurrying from the room.

Lord Belham glanced once at the cover and tore open the seal. The letter had come from Carlisle. Ah, so the small Lord Dunraven and his governess were successfully being pursued. But who the devil was this young man with Miss Drake? He was very completely described: black hair, blue eyes, handsome, the high-handed style of a gentleman. Yet the letter contained an extremely unlikely tale to account for the fellow's presence. According to the neighbors at the Manse he had been found washed up on the beach and was remarkably proficient with a pistol. Would that prove awkward or convenient?

The marquess tossed the letter into the fire and stared thoughtfully for a moment at the flames. Devil take the dowager countess! Lady Dunraven was a mad old witch! Lord Belham closed his eyes for a moment. By God, she had cost him dearly enough! How tempting was the thought of revenge! At least the child was coming toward London, thus every day brought him closer to the home of his new guardian.

There would be something very delightful about floating slowly south through the green spring countryside of England, the round rumps of the tow horses steadily leading the way, if Prudence did not have to pretend that she was married to Hal.

A day and a half out of Runcorn, Prudence sat quite comfortably on a cushion at the back of *The White Lady,* mending one of Bobby's little muslin suits. Sweet, warm sunshine flooded her perch. For the moment Bobby was playing safely next to her on the tiny deck, building and destroying innumerable castles made from small pieces of clay.

Sam's son Willie rode the first of the tow horses, which were harnessed in tandem. The boy was about nine years old, yellow-headed and shy, and Bobby had shared a bed with Willie near his father in the small cabin last night. Meanwhile Hal and Prudence had indeed been given a private spot. Their host had made them a sleeping nook at the front of the barge amongst some bales of cloth he had thrown in on top of his cargo. Only canvas formed a frail roof between their bed and the elements. They were to be nestled in cotton like chicks in the nest.

But with silent courtesy, when they had tied up for the night, Hal had allowed Prudence to go to bed without him. She'd had no idea what he was doing until at least an hour later, when she had felt him slide in beside her, chilled and damp, and realized that he had been swimming in the canal until he was exhausted. Yet when she awoke in the morning, he was already gone.

Prudence glanced at Bobby and felt the rush of love and protection that she always did. How could a child be so absorbed in the moment? Bobby seemed to have neither regrets about the past, nor fears for the future. Earlier that morning he had ridden on the tow horse with Willie. When this had first been suggested, Prudence had objected firmly. But Hal, who was learning the correct feel of the tiller, had laughed at her and winked at Sam, their host.

"When we have a lad of our own, wife, then you may have your say. But Bobby is my boy. And I say he may ride the horse with Willie if he likes."

Bobby had crowed with pleasure, and Prudence had been forced to bite her lip and concede. But how dare Hal take advantage of their masquerade in such an outrageous fashion?

Bobby's safety was her responsibility! Even when Hal leaned closer and whispered in her ear, it did not mollify her feelings.

"Never fear, angel. These horses may look like giants, but they are more gentle than kittens, and Willie has a fine understanding with them. Bobby will come to no harm."

And of course he had not. Bobby had ridden for half an hour on his high perch, clutching both hands in the harness, until Hal said that it was enough, and then he had happily come back to the barge.

No, it was Hal himself who was the prime cause of Prudence's discomfort now. For Hal was either stripped to the waist as he worked with Sam at the constant daily tasks—the ongoing painting and repair to the vessel; the polishing of the brass; the care of the tow horses; the strenuous help to the lock-keepers working the machinery which opened and closed the locks on the canal—or his shirt was left carelessly open at the neck with the sleeves rolled to the armpits. Either way, it revealed far too much firm, masculine flesh. Jamie's roughly delivered bruises were already fading from Hal's skin, and Prudence was mortified that she had noticed.

But how could she think of much else, except Hal? She was every minute presented with his physical beauty. She had never before been aware of how enticing a man's body could be. And surely he was shamelessly flaunting himself! He climbed, laughing, about the boat or leapt carelessly up onto the bank, with the ease of an athlete. Prudence had never been so close to a man going freely about a man's work before, or at least not a young man with muscles like silk, like Hal's. To see him move was more captivating than any measure in a ball room. The family friends of her childhood and her rough-and-tumble brothers seemed clumsy and homespun in comparison. Above his sleek shoulders, his hair, now far too long, ran back in a dark mane from his fine-boned face. He seemed always merry, always relaxed. When they had a moment alone together, he teased her unmercifully, yet how carefully he had allowed Prudence to maintain her modesty when they had been obliged to crawl together into the tiny bed provided for them! But how was she to cope with this intimacy with him, day after day, night after night?

"Your wife is a shy lass, isn't she?" asked Sam, jerking his head back over his shoulder to indicate Prudence.

Hal glanced up. He was strapping down a loose cord near the front of the narrow boat. Sam had left the tiller for a moment and come climbing up over the cargo to talk to him.

"Is she?" asked Hal.

"Aye, she's as skittish as a filly that's not been broken to harness. I've seen her draw back from you when you pass by, yet she's very aware of you. She's nervous, belike—and with a fine set-up, comely young lad like yourself! Now, you'll not take amiss some advice from an old man, would you?"

Hal looked down to cover his laughter. "No, sir. Indeed not."

"Then you must court her, lad, like you did before you were wed. Especially when you were married in a hurry at Gretna. For all she's your wife, and now you can take your rights when you please, you must soften her all the time, not just when you want her—like gentling a horse. Give her a kiss or a pat when you pass her. Let her know that you think she's a pretty thing. She'll be moving into your arms of her own accord then, soon enough."

Hal straightened up. He could just see the glossy curve of Prudence's blond hair as she bent her head over the sewing. There was no laughter at all in his voice as he replied, "I do think she's a pretty thing, sir. I'd not have married her otherwise, would I? In fact I think she is beautiful. But I believe she has no idea of it. She thinks she is meek and plain, and doesn't have enough color. She has no idea that she is a woman to inspire passion."

* * *

As the words floated back soft and clear on the quiet water, Prudence felt scarlet color wash up from her neck to stain her face. Oh, dear Lord! *A woman to inspire passion?* The needle jabbed into her finger, and she brought the bead of blood to her mouth and frantically sucked it away. Oh, gracious heavens! Hal believed she was desirable! Did he mean to seduce her when he kissed her? Was that why he had done it? Had he meant to gentle her, like a horse?

She stopped working for a moment and blinked the tears away from her eyes. Bobby left his blocks and clambered up past the cabin onto the canvas cargo cover. *In fact I think she is beautiful.* Had he meant her to hear it? With a desperate attempt at calm, Prudence stood up and shook out her skirt. Then she turned around to put Bobby's mended suit back into the cabin. Sam was clambering back to the tiller, and Hal was still busy with the rope. As he flexed his shoulders, light and shadow ran in beautiful patterns over the muscles of his back. He laughed at something which Bobby said to him and squatted down to speak to the child. Every moment was lithe, and frighteningly masculine.

Prudence hurried into the tiny cabin and closed the door, her breath coming far too fast beneath her prim brown bodice, and sank down onto the narrow bench opposite the tiny stove and the clever dresser with its drop-down table top. She buried her face in her hands. *Who was he? Who was he?*

"Which would you like, angel? Darkness and ease, or light and exercise?" Prudence looked around. Hal was standing at the door of the cabin looking in. To her relief he had put on his shirt. "We are about to pass through a tunnel, known when it was built, according to Sam, as the eighth wonder of the world. It's over a mile and a half long and will take about two hours to get through. The horses must go over the top. Shall we walk with them?''

Prudence stood up and stepped out to join him on the tiny deck. Ahead of them the landscape climbed away to form a ridge of high ground. There seemed to be no possible path at all for the flat, meandering waterway. But it ran straight toward the hill and disappeared into an impossibly tiny opening. A tunnel. Several narrow boats were lined up along the bank waiting their turn to enter it, for it allowed only one foot of clearance on each side and a string of boats was coming through the other way. Sam maneuvered *The White Lady* into the bank to wait her turn.

Prudence watched with amazement as a boat slowly emerged from the opening. An entire crew of men were lying on their backs on each side of her, pushing the narrow boat along with their feet against the walls of the tunnel. At her questioning look, Hal told her, ''It's called 'legging through', and I'm going to leave it to the professionals. Sam will hire these fellows to take *The White Lady* to the other side, and while she disappears underground, we shall walk over the top with the horses.''

She didn't want to be with him, but the prospect of being underground for two long, dark hours was far worse. Yet it almost seemed that Hal understood her feelings for he walked ahead with the horses and allowed her to trail along behind with Bobby. It spared her his teasing company, but it did not spare her the sight of him, striding across the heath as if with no care in the world.

After they rejoined *The White Lady* and reattached the tow line, Prudence stayed alone in the little cabin, preparing the evening's meal in the neat, tight quarters, everything to hand without moving a step. That night they arrived in Stoke-on-Trent, where the cargo was unloaded and replaced with crates of finished pottery. Thus it was very late when they finally tied up at a canal-side inn with several other boats. Prudence crawled alone into her little bed. Hal had disappeared into the town, and did not reappear until morning. *Why was she not glad?*

* * *

The next day they traveled steadily south-east in the broad, shallow valley of the Trent, through Stone and the Haywards toward Rugeley. The simple repetitive tasks of the canal occupied the day, and Hal talked with Sam about what he had learned in Stoke: Napoleon had escaped Elba and landed in France. Prudence barely listened to the news. Soon *The White Lady* would arrive safely in Oxford, and she would send word to her sister. She would never see Hal again, then this long, slow torment would be over, and plain, uncomplicated Prudence Drake could regain her common sense and her equilibrium. But once again, Hal joined her that night after she had undressed and slipped into the tiny bed. As he had done two nights before, first he had gone for a long swim in the cold canal so that his hair was still damp. Though a chill emanated from his skin, beneath it he seemed to burn as if with a fever. Prudence lay with her back to him, her eyes tightly shut, and pretended to be asleep.

"I think I would very much like a payment, angel," he said softly, as if to himself, with a wry, dreamy edge to his voice. "For God's sake, I am working so damned hard, and getting nothing for it but your frowns and disapproval. Just one sweet payment. A very gentle, innocent, friendly payment, if you like. Just once more before you disappear into your sister's respectable household. But, devil take me, better yet, I think I would like a kiss, freely and passionately given, and offered from the heart."

Prudence sat up, drawing the blankets up under her chin.

"It's not fair," she said firmly.

"Oh, dear God!" Hal slipped instantly from the bed and sat down on the edge of a canvas-wrapped bale. To her surprise he put his head in his hands, while his shoulders shook as if with silent laughter.

"It's not fair! I did not ask you to come with us from the Manse!"

"Forgive my careless words, I pray! I thought you were asleep!"

"I didn't agree to any payment! You work our passage out of some idle whim of your own and from your own free will."

Hal dropped his hands and looked up at her. In the shifting light she couldn't clearly see his expression, but the long black hair curled back from his pale, moon-washed face like the slick coat of some wild beast. There was the edge of something close to anger—or close to despair—in his voice. "And so I do, angel. Forget that I spoke. It was only the folly of fatigue. Go to sleep."

"Sam is becoming suspicious that I don't behave as a fond wife should, isn't he?"

Prudence was completely unprepared for the bitter edge to his voice. "It doesn't matter. If Sam puts us off because our marriage is in ruins, we shall no doubt find another narrow boat, though it would be easier to stay with him as far as Oxford, of course."

"And after Oxford?"

"Let us get so far! In the meantime can't we do a little playacting? For Bobby's sake? You don't need to kiss me again, but for God's sake, couldn't you meet my eyes once in a while, or smile at me when I sit down to dinner, or speak to me without being spoken to first?"

Her fingers were closed tensely on the blanket. She felt wary, even afraid. "Perhaps."

"You don't believe in subterfuge, Miss Drake, even in a good cause?"

"I shall try to be more friendly to you in front of Sam and Willie. I'm sorry if I have seemed cool, but it's not a very amiable situation, is it? To pretend to be wed, when we are strangers!"

He laughed with a sudden, strong passion. "*Strangers?* You are a sane, unpretentious, and benevolent person, with a real existence in a real world. It is only by accident that you find yourself in such an odd predicament. Only I am the stranger—

with nothing but a head full of verses and book-learning, and
a body with unknown skills I discover daily—I can shoot, I
can box, and I know how to handle the ribbons. But I don't
seem to have any personal history or even a name!''

"You remembered the name of your brother, didn't you?
John?''

"Ah, yes, so I did. But the name has no face and I can't
place the feelings connected to it.''

"And a woman's name!''

There was the edge of a deep raillery to his voice. "Yes,
Helena! I have dreamt about her, but I don't know who she is.
In the meantime, if I see myself in a mirror an intruder stares
back and wonders what the devil he is doing there. My own
face shifts meaning with my mood, as if I changed shape with
the tides. I can't know what I might do next, because there's
no anchor in what I have done before. Nothing but confusion
glares at me out of a mirror! Whereas when you look in the
glass, you see the familiar features of Miss Prudence Drake.
You have grown so used to them that you hardly notice the
way your eyes are sometimes green and sometimes brown, or
that your eyelashes are two shades darker than your brows, or
that if you smile there is the most enchantingly severe dimple
in your left cheek. You only worry in case your hair isn't parted
quite perfectly, or if your mouth is not just a little too straight.
And the lady behind that face is someone you even believe
you understand! What do you want out of life, Miss Drake?''

Prudence stared at him in genuine surprise. The breath
seemed stuck in her throat. "What do you mean?'' It came out
as a hoarse whisper.

"How do you envisage your future?''

"I don't know. I am a governess. I am very happy taking
care of Bobby.''

"Which is a form of slavery. You will never earn enough
to gain independence. Old age will await you with the degradation and pain of real poverty, or the mortification and pitfalls
of being taken in by charitable relatives. Meanwhile, although

you are a lady, you will always be trapped in a humiliating position half-way between the family and the servants, belonging nowhere. There will never be love, except that of children, but Bobby will go to school in a few years and break your heart. Then what? Another post taking care of another child, until your heart breaks again? Don't you want a husband and children of your own?''

Prudence felt desperate, as if the future were closing about her in the dark. "I don't think about it. Governesses don't usually have those kinds of choices. What about your future? What do you want?''

"How can I know?'' He laughed, but his voice almost betrayed him. Beneath the light, cynical amusement Prudence sensed something quite different. "How can a man without a past plan a future? Unless we know where we've been, how can we make sense of where we're going? For all I know, my future lies in Newgate among the debtors, or the thieves, or the murderers.''

"Stuff and nonsense,'' said Prudence with more conviction than she felt. "If you had murdered someone you would know it—in your bones. You would feel the enormity of it every day weighing down your soul.''

Hal stood up. He was wearing only a pair of thin muslin drawers which covered him from waist to knee. With shock Prudence realized that they were the fine undergarments of a gentleman, as her father had worn under his knee breeches. The three-inch waistband was tightened at the back with tapes; three small vertical buttons fastened in front. Since they were only a little damp, Hal must have swum naked and put them on afterward. Prudence hurried her gaze up over his lithe midriff and chest, so enchantingly different from her own, as a hot flush burned her cheeks and washed through her belly. She tried desperately not to notice, when he bent to slip from their little tent, how the damp fabric below the knotted tapes clung to the hard, rounded, muscled shape of him, every bit as revealing and far more enticing than the nakedness of her dreams.

She gulped. "Oh, goodness!" she said under her breath.

Hal stood silhouetted against the dark willow-covered banks of the canal, as lovely as a god or the silkie of the fairy tale. As the moonlight caught his features she could see that he grinned at her and that this time the amusement was genuine, though it was only a riotous, wild mockery directed at himself.

"And if I am a Casanova, Miss Drake, with a trail of ruined women and bastard children behind me, would I feel the enormity of that, too?"

Without removing the unmentionable garment this time, he dived back into the water.

Prudence forced herself out of the warm bed, gathering the voluminous folds of her cream muslin nightgown in one hand. She leaned over the low rail of the barge. "Are you mad? You will die of cold!"

His head moved sleekly through the water, like a seal's, as he swam back to her.

"Would you care, angel?"

He dived and disappeared for a moment, before surfacing again in a different spot.

"Of course I should care if you made yourself ill!"

Spreading his hands in the water in an exaggerated gesture of surrender, he laughed up at her, his black hair running water over his face. "Because how then would you get Bobby to your sister's?"

His strong, long-fingered hands closed on the rail and Hal slipped out of the canal, water streaming down his body.

Prudence held up a towel which he had apparently left there and with a burning confusion of emotion watched his neat movements as he dried himself. "Well, of course that's a consideration—but only for Bobby's sake!"

He toweled vigorously at his hair. "And is there nothing you want from me for your own sake, angel? You have been avoiding me as if I carried the plague! For God's sake, seize the day! Take the opportunity to discover something outside of the schoolroom. How do you know if the chance will ever come again? Why don't you use me while I'm here?''

She felt frantic, trapped by his forcefulness. "Use you? How?''

"We could see what we could learn from each other." He reached out a cold hand and touched her cheek. The gentleness of it was infinitely disarming. "With honesty, even with affection, perhaps. I don't ask for your virtue, for God's sake! 'Be not coy, but use your time, / And while ye may, go marry.' Or at least try a little harmless courting. Was what happened at the waterfall so dreadful? I felt your response then and again in Gretna Green, deny it though you may!''

"You think I should kiss you again!''

"Maybe. After all, you survived twice, didn't you?''

"But what would we discover, sir?''

He turned with a desperate violence that left her shaken. "Whether I am really a rake, perhaps. How the devil can I know? But a lady should be able to tell!''

"So you will use me to find out something about yourself? What on earth can I learn?''

"Whatever you desire! You are in charge, madam. Wouldn't you like to know something about pleasure? The delight of a caress, a shared touch. Remember, we are married!''

"No, we are not!'' said Prudence, desperately. "That business in Gretna Green was a mockery! I don't imagine I shall ever marry.''

"Oh, yes, you will.'' He had taken the loose end of her long plait, and was idly running it over the palm of one hand and sliding the knobby braids through his fingers. "You just don't know why you must. Have you never felt your own hair? It's so soft, like the down on a chick. Close your eyes and just feel.'' He took her hand and turned it palm up, then brushed it softly with the silky blond plait. "Now that is a harmless enough pleasure, isn't it, Prudence?''

"Don't!'' she said blindly, closing her fingers over the delicious sensation, and tearing her plait out of his hand. "I don't want to learn anything from you!"

Hal turned away and slid to his haunches, dropping his damp head to his knees. He was quite still, his hands pressed over his eyes and mouth, the curve of his back sculpted in the moonlight.

Prudence glared down at him. "And don't laugh at me! I know I seem foolish and ignorant to someone like you."

"Oh, dear God, angel! I am far from laughter. Though the amazing absurdity of my situation brings me daily amusement, of course."

As he lifted his head, Prudence saw his face in the moonlight. *Like Abou Hassan, I might believe I am the caliph, for I'm damned if I know otherwise.* Abou Hassan, the young man of Baghdad, carried in the night to the bed of the Caliph, Harun-al-Rashid, in the *Arabian Nights.* Hal was ravaged, not by laughter but by despair, and the frost of it seemed to have sunk to his bones. Prudence felt hot tears slide down her cheeks. Without thinking she tugged a blanket from their bed and wrapped it about his shoulders.

Yet as she did so, Hal caught her hand in his own and pulled her down into his arms.

"Don't offer largesse to a rogue unless you mean it, angel," he said fiercely, tucking her with him into a fold of the blanket. Then he caught her face in his palm and turned her mouth up to his.

Chapter 7

His cold mouth pressed against hers, drinking in her warmth, plundering her generosity. A kiss with a searing depth of passion. Prudence was caught against his naked chest in a tangle of cream muslin, her breasts crushed against him, while the ice melted away in the flame where their lips met. Through the thin fabric of her nightgown an intense fire burned from his skin into hers. They fell back together against the canvas while Hal's lean fingers ran boldly over her shoulders and down her back, following the curves of her waist and hips. He kissed her neck and the corner of her jaw, then ran his tongue down to the pulse at the base of her throat and suckled there, like a child. Prudence felt the enchantment of it, the rapture, and moaned softly into his damp hair. It was so very, very, lovely!

She did not know she returned his embrace until she discovered for the first time the delectable feel of a man's muscles under her hands and the softness of the fine down that curled over his chest. He was so firm and smooth! It was so delightful to touch him! She wanted to discover everything about him, all of his mysteries and all of his subtlety. With her hands and with her body, Prudence longed to know how and why he was so different from her, to discover all of his powerful, masculine secrets.

"What the hell is all this damned muslin?" he murmured with a soft rumble of amusement as he bit gently at the lobe of her ear. His hands were caught up in the voluminous folds of her night rail.

And Prudence knew to her shame that she wanted to tear open the buttons at the neck of her nightgown and let his sensitive fingers explore where they would. Her breasts ached; surely only his touch would assuage it? At the shock of the thought, she went rigid.

Hal released her, but holding her firmly by the shoulders kissed her once in the center of her forehead.

"Sweet, foolish Prudence." He was breathless, but healing laughter seemed to well up in him once again. "Your name belies you! There is nothing you can learn from a rake, dear kind soul, except the road to ruin! I wish you would slap me as hard as you can, marry a fine upstanding fellow with a brace of hounds and a house in the country, and send him after me with a double-barreled shooting piece! I deserve death in a ditch for this, and the wind wailing over me."

"I don't understand!" It was almost a sob.

There was a gentleness in his voice which threatened to break her heart. "Don't try, please, to understand! Go to bed! I shall sleep outside."

Hal pushed her into the little nest under the canvas, and pulled the covers over her before he thrust back out into the cold night. He picked up the abandoned blanket and dropped away out of sight. Prudence silently cried herself to sleep as cold water slapped in a slow rhythm against the boat.

The next morning Hal walked along the towpath with the two boys and the horses, leaving Prudence on the narrow boat. In the clear, warm, innocent light of morning, the entire encoun-

ter of the previous night felt like a dream. Hal had treated her
with a warm, gentle courtesy over breakfast, putting her at ease
and allowing her almost to believe that it had never happened.
Yet she had no desire to talk with Sam who stood silently at
the tiller, so she sat at the front of the boat and—for Bobby's
sake—did her best to act the dutiful wife.

Prudence didn't want to meet his eyes, or allow herself to
see anything of what he was feeling, but she was mending
Hal's jacket.

*You hardly notice the way your eyes are sometimes green
and sometimes brown, or that your eyelashes are two shades
darker than your brows.*

There was no decent mirror on the narrow boat. And anyway,
it was nonsense. The practiced, deceitful nonsense of a rake.
Prudence blindly stabbed the needle back toward the rent in
his coat, and something hard turned it aside.

*Or that if you smile there is the most enchantingly severe
dimple in your left cheek.*

How could he! She had been perfectly content with her life
as a governess before she had found him, before he had opened
those eyes that reflected the sky and thought to amuse himself
by tormenting her. She pulled the needle out of his jacket, then
rammed it back. The needle struck the obstruction again. How
very odd! Prudence stopped and felt carefully along the seam.
Yes, there! A quite distinct small lump in the fabric. This was
the jacket that Hal had been wearing on the beach, the sailor's
jacket that no gentleman would dream of wearing. The jacket
he had worn with the rough trousers—although now she knew
that beneath them lay the underthings of a gentleman. Nothing
about him made sense. Why on earth would he have lumps in
his clothing? Without compunction Prudence picked apart the
stitches along the seam. In seconds she had uncovered a tiny,
tight roll of oilskin.

With fingers that shook she unrolled it. Inside was a slip of
paper with a set of odd symbols neatly written across one side.

Some were letters or numbers, others were signs that seemed totally occult to her.

She had not known what or who he was, but she had been enthralled, hadn't she? As fascinated by him as if he really were an alien creature from a fairy tale, the silkie who shed his skin to rear up at the foot of a lady's bed in the shape of a man, then leave her with child and bereft. The paper burned in her fingers like a message from Tir-nan-og, the magical land of youth. The writing might as well have been the witless scribbling of the wee folk, for none of the symbols made sense. But sensible Miss Drake did not believe in fairy tales, and she knew that the paper must have a far more sinister meaning than that.

Prudence clutched her hands together in her lap. This was proof! Proof that Hal was indeed something extraordinary. For ordinary people did not mysteriously appear on beaches in Scotland when no regular passenger ship had gone missing. Ordinary people did not wear the underwear and boots of the wealthy with the outer garments of the poor. And ordinary people did not carry secret messages concealed in their clothes when they came from France. She tried to remember exactly what Hal had been telling Sam. For it was obvious that the paper was in code, and it seemed that Hal had brought it just as Napoleon was leaving Elba. Which meant that Hal was either a spy or a traitor, or very possibly both.

She glanced up at him where he walked ahead with the boys. With those elegant, clever, gentleman's hands he took Bobby around the waist and tossed him onto the back of one of the horses. The child's squeal of delight echoed across the water. Prudence quickly folded the paper and slipped it inside her own pocket, until she could decide what on earth to do about this appalling discovery.

Three days later, in a deathly silence broken only by the insistent ticking of the large clock on the mantelpiece, Lord

Belham received the news that his quarry had dropped off the face of the earth. They had been seen last in Liverpool—and then nothing. No carriage, either private or public, had carried a woman, a boy, and a black-haired man south. His agent would swear his soul on it. An ever-widening net of questioning at coaching inns had uncovered no sign of the fugitives. Surely Miss Drake could not have carried the boy north again?

Liverpool was a major port. God help him if she had boarded a ship and taken to sea and the child with her!

The marquess studied the letter from his agent once more. The man was thorough and knew his task. Miss Prudence Drake, daughter of a respectable and canny Scot, had earned her own living since she was seventeen. She had siblings, orphaned and scattered about the globe. Apparently her upbringing had been dour and restricted. Everything pointed to the hypothesis that she was naive and trusting. Did she trust this mysterious black-haired man to rescue her? Miss Drake no doubt cared for the child and desired his safety, but was she capable of protecting him?

Belham looked up and cursed aloud, shattering the quiet of his dark study. Devil take this black-haired man, whoever he was! By all accounts he was careless and cavalier, but he had somehow managed to secrete little Lord Dunraven and his governess—and so well that trained spies had lost track of them. So the dissolute Marquess of Belham was going to have to take a hand in this damnable business himself! He stood up, then crossed to his sideboard, his movements as lithe as a stalking cat's, and poured himself a brandy.

If the man with black hair was indeed a gentleman, it was likely that he was a member of one of the London clubs. Had anyone gone missing? Was there a family concerned over the whereabouts of a son or a brother? And he was rumored to have come from France—was there anyone who was known to have gone there, and was expected back? Thank God the agent had sent such a very complete description, for there was something in it that rang a bell. Perhaps the identity of the fellow wouldn't be so hard to discover, and that might determine where the hell he was likely to be going—and the little heir to a castle and a fortune with him.

For God's sake! *The life of a five-year-old hangs by a slender enough thread.* He must find the child as soon as possible!

There was a knock at the door, and Lord Belham turned around in some annoyance. "Come!"

The slow ripple of water slapped gently against the narrow boat, gently rocking Prudence where she sat on her cushions outside the cabin with the mending—one of Sam's shirts lay in her lap. They had stopped, somewhere on the Oxford Canal, with the rich green fields and budding trees of England spreading away on both sides of the water. Prudence was not aware that their slow progress had halted, or that the air was heavy with the promise of the oncoming evening. The needle lay still in her fingers. She was agonizing over whether she had done the right thing.

If Hal carried treasonous messages, someone in government had to be told, didn't they? Prudence had a brother in His Majesty's Navy. He had written her long letters about the fight against the French. Even though there was an uneasy truce with Napoleon right now, William's very life might depend upon her acting with resolution. The message might have contained information about Napoleon's plans, even an invasion of the south coast, or a sudden strike against the allies in Belgium. William would expect her to follow the call of patriotic duty, whatever her personal feelings about it might be. So before she could change her mind, Prudence had folded the paper with its occult symbols and odd collection of letters and numbers inside a letter to Admiral Rafter in London—because William had mentioned him once, and she did not know the name of any other person in government. As soon as *The White Lady* tied up that night, Prudence had slipped ashore and posted her letter.

And felt like a snail for not telling Hal what she had done.

For if she had shown him the coded message, it might have jogged his memory of who he was and why he had been traveling to Scotland, and cleared him of that agony which she had witnessed all those nights ago, when he had kissed her. But what if he remembered that he was a French spy? And what if she had been so willing and so wanton in the arms of a traitor to his country?

A slow, deep burn began to flood up her neck as she remembered it. And remember it she did, every day. Hal had promised to teach her something, but what she had learned had woken a restless longing that would leave her never content again. Plain, prim, and proper Miss Prudence Drake, douce Scots governess, had discovered that she was no better than a strumpet.

It made it very hard to meet his eyes in casual conversation, or act with the affection that a wife should so that Sam would not become suspicious. Especially when Hal had greeted her across the breakfast table the next morning with dark circles under his eyes.

"Whatever ails you this morning, lad?" asked Sam brightly. "Spent the night with the night mare riding your conscience?"

Hal had looked back at him and laughed. "Bad dreams, sir? Indeed, my dreams are of beautiful women. Why would you think they would rob me of sleep?"

Prudence knew with certainty that Hal had gone straight from her arms to dream again about the mysterious Helena.

Thank God that Hal was spending most of his time with Bobby, teaching the boy to ride and to swim. Every day Bobby rode the great tow horses, learning a good seat and a secure balance. Each evening the lithe, strong man and the fragile child dropped together into the canal, and Bobby shrieked with delight in the silver sprays of water splashed up by their games. Bobby was already able to float by himself, and hang onto the side of the narrow boat and kick. Meanwhile, whenever they must be together, Hal had been gentle with her, and teasing, and patient to a fault, but Prudence could not forget that she had felt such a burning passion in his arms.

She had let a man awaken her—like Sleeping Beauty—with a kiss, and then she had stolen his coded paper and betrayed him. It made her hot with misery. It was as if the blazing sun and the open barge left her with no place to hide. Prudence closed her eyes and dropped her head over Sam's torn shirt, knowing her face would soon be as red as the painted poppies on the cabin wall.

"You would seem to have caught too much sunshine, angel," said that cultured voice with its enchanting edge of humor. "You should wear your bonnet when England decides to surprise us with a heat wave."

Prudence looked up to find Hal had climbed onto the small tiller deck and was smiling down at her.

He dropped down on his haunches beside her. "I had hoped I was forgiven," he said quietly. "It has been three days."

"We are stopped!" exclaimed Prudence, noticing the stillness. "Why?"

"We are almost to Banbury—where there is a major boat yard and the toll gate is locked at eight o'clock sharp."

"Where shall we stop for the night, then?" Prudence deliberately took the way out. They had not shared a personal conversation since that eventful night, and she was determined to keep it that way.

"Here. Sam has taken the boys with him to take care of the horses. There is stabling at a small inn just around the next bend, but the berths there are all filled. We shall stay tied up along the canal bank, as we have done every night since I kissed you and you kissed me back. And once again I shall sleep on the bank, rolled in a blanket under the hedge like a gypsy, lest I ravish you in your sleep."

So he would not let her escape it! Prudence stood up and looked after the retreating figures of their skipper and the two boys. They had unharnessed the horses and were leading them away. She had been left alone on the narrow boat with Hal, while she dreamed away the moments during which she could have avoided it. A kingfisher dived with a sudden flash of blue into the water, startling her.

"If you were a gentleman you would not talk of what happened," she said.

"We must talk about it, angel. Sam thinks I have been beating you! He told me he would not keep such a villain aboard if I did not apologize and win back your smiles. Was it so very dreadful to kiss me?"

Prudence whirled about to face him as the kingfisher rose from the water, a small silver fish in its beak. "You are a villain! A rake and a villain!"

Hal stepped up onto the roof of the cabin and lay down, casually stretching out his long legs. "Is that why you blush like a rose when you think of me, angel?"

"I'm not blushing. It is hot and the sun is too strong, that is all! I think I shall suffocate if it does not cool off soon!"

"Then you should come for a swim. In the canal. It would calm all your passions and soothe your wrath."

The kingfisher had perched on a branch overhanging the water. In one quick movement the bird turned the small fish in its beak and swallowed it. "I can't swim!" There was a note close to panic in her voice.

He supported his cheek on one hand, his weight on his elbow. Dark hair curled over his fingertips. "But the water is cool and refreshing and kind. I could support you and you could bathe away all of the hot, sticky antagonism you have felt toward me for the last several days, and the heat of the sun which has poisoned your bones, and the difficulty of not washing as much as you have wanted. Slide into the water, angel. It feels very good."

"I told you I can't swim. It's completely out of the question!"

"Why? Do you think you can't trust me?"

If only he weren't so beautiful, looking into her eyes with

that searching harebell gaze! "After what happened? I know I can't trust you!"

"Because I kissed you and you liked it? For God's sake, I should have thought if there's one thing that I proved then, it's that you can trust me, and that in spite of all your accusations and my own fears, I am not a rake."

He could reach out a hand and catch her to him if he so wanted. He could kiss her again, there on the small deck with the sun beating down, and she would not be able to stop him. "How on earth do you arrive at that conclusion?"

"Because, my dear Miss Drake, a rake would not have stopped as I did, when I did, and thus you would no longer be in possession of your virtue." He sat up and looked away into the willows, the sun casting a strong shadow under his jaw. "I wanted to go on! I wanted it with every fiber of my being, for God's sake. You are an enchantment to my senses, angel. But I did not—even though you would have let me. If, after that, you think that you cannot trust me, then I'd very much like to know what is your definition of trust."

"Do you trust me?" she said miserably.

He looked down at her and smiled. "Absolutely."

She felt the enormous weight of her betrayal of him like a collar of iron, as his harebell eyes watched her with nothing but concern. "Why?"

"Because you are open and honorable and kind, and would do nothing underhanded or cruel."

"You cannot know that!" wailed Prudence, feeling a great depth of misery.

Hal leant down and caught her by the hand. "Yes, I can. I would trust you with my life, angel. For I know I have already trusted you with my heart."

She knew her face was scarlet, and her pulse hammered uncomfortably in her throat as if it would choke her. "This is madness!"

He turned her fingers over in his and looked at them. Then he raised them to his lips and kissed the back of her knuckles,

courteously, gently, yet with a thrumming of underlying tension
that shook her to the core. "Yes, I know it is. I did not plan
to tell you, and I demand that you not answer me, but I am in
love with you. I'm damned sorry."

Prudence snatched back her hand. She felt lost, bereft of
direction. "Why sorry?"

He ran both hands back through his black hair. "Because I
cannot ask you to marry me when I don't know who I am, can
I? I should not in honor have declared myself, for you are
left without any possible response. Therefore, don't reply. Just
know that I care for you, that I shan't let any harm befall you,
and that you can trust me. Is that good enough?"

"I don't know what to say!"

"Say nothing." He smiled with that warm, irrepressible
humor, but a dark shadow lay beneath it. "Perhaps many years
from now, when you are sitting at your hearth with that bold
fellow with the double-barreled gun beside you and your children snug in their beds upstairs, you will tell him about me
and laugh a little over it. 'I kissed a fellow who came out of
the sea', you will say, 'for he was a madman and I was sorry
for him. It seemed to be a bit of a risk, but indeed it was no
risk at all.'"

"How can you say there was no risk?"

"Because you were never in danger."

If he knew the unsteady state of her heart, he would not have
said it! "I wasn't a person to know much about risk and danger
before I met you."

And suddenly he laughed. "Thus says the lady who flees
Scotland alone with her five-year-old pupil, though a sinister
one-eyed man tails her and a marquess wants the lad dead! Yet
you think of yourself as so staid, don't you? For God's sake,
you have a natural talent to discover and devour the world,
angel. Seize the day! This is your chance to try the delights of
new ventures, before the real world crowds back in on you
with its constricting demands and expectations of propriety!
We have another day, right now, and have wasted three. Let

us seize this one! What else have you always longed to do, besides really kiss a man, but never dared, Miss Drake?''

''I don't know! Please, don't do this! I don't want to try new things!''

''But new things are God's gift to our dreary days. And it is devilish hot! Let us swim, Miss Drake. You can trust me and you can also trust the water. There's no danger.''

''I should be afraid!''

''You said you had suffered from too much sun. Come, this beneficent liquid will cool you. You can trust me. I have proved it, haven't I?''

Prudence closed her eyes. Oh, dear Lord! When she had been guilty of the most dreadful betrayal! Although she had not told Admiral Rafter where she and Hal were or where they were heading, it was possible that by sending the coded note to London she had put Hal in mortal danger. Prudence felt she deserved to be punished, and she knew without any question that she must demonstrate to Hal that she trusted him—with her life, if necessary. She must make amends for what she had done. Because, after all, whoever he was, she loved him with a desperation that was threatening to destroy her!

''How can I go in the water in my gown?'' she asked, ashamed that her voice trembled.

''It doesn't matter. It will dry.''

Hal dropped down from the tiny flat roof and stood beside her. In a few rapid movements he had stripped off his shirt and boots, and stood naked from the waist up before her: magnificent, beautiful, and far too inviting.

''Come!'' He held out his hands.

Prudence put her fingers into his and he helped her to sit on the bow rail. Then he knelt at her feet and began to unbutton her boots. It was disturbingly intimate. She reached down a hand to stop him and did it herself. Then she carefully reached up under her skirts and peeled off her stockings. She dropped her little jacket next to her boots on the deck, and stood up, clothed only in her thin muslin dress, her arms bare to the bright air, and watched Hal drop silently over the rail into the water. He ducked and turned over in the water like a seal, then he held up his hands to her.

"Don't jump. Just sit on the rail and slide into the canal. I will catch you."

The water brushed over her bare feet like cool, damp silk. Hal reached up both hands and caught her by the waist, then he eased her into the canal beside him. It was colder than she had expected and she gasped. An icy clutch of fear made her grasp at his shoulders. The tears that came to her eyes were purely from panic.

"It's all right, angel. Hold onto me if you like, but I won't let you go."

Prudence felt his strong arm around her waist, and the steady movement of his legs as he thrust them rhythmically in the water, keeping them both afloat. She frantically clasped both arms about his neck. His firm, muscled shoulders were slick and cool against her bare skin. Her skirts coiled up around her legs as her body was crushed into his. She bit hard at her lip to prevent herself from crying out. But Hal did not let her go and he did not let the water touch her face, though his own black hair streamed wet over his shoulders. Slowly she began to relax and allow herself to feel the wonder of it. The soft water and the hard strength of the man who supported her.

"Now, angel, let go of my neck and lie back. I shall take care of you."

She called on all of her courage and slipped her hands away from his neck. Hal supported her easily, one hand under her head and the other beneath her waist as she fell back against him in the water.

"I can't!" she gasped.

"Yes, you can! Arch your back, tuck in your chin, and float. I have you safe, I shan't let go."

Prudence did as she was told, her breath coming in short, nervous gasps, but Hal's arms were still under her, and slowly she began to relax.

"There," he said. "It is easy. You are weightless like the mermaids on the sea-foam . . . and it is cool . . . and nothing can harm you."

Prudence closed her eyes, lest he should see the tears of wonder suddenly welling up in them. She was floating!

Lord Belham had to repeat the command. "Come!"

A fresh young face, remarkably well-scrubbed and with a high starched collar framing red cheeks, peered respectfully at him from the doorway. "Glad to find you at home, my lord. I trust I don't disturb you? I have been sent with an urgent task from the Admiralty."

It was young Wilson, one of the lads who ran messages for the ministers.

"I am all ears, sir. Pray sit. Would you care for a brandy?"

Wilson colored up to his eyebrows. "I could hardly presume so far, my lord."

"Nonsense." Lord Belham smiled. "Here, it is excellent brandy—it will teach you to develop an educated palate. Now, what charming assignment do you have for me this time?"

"Admiral Rafter received an odd note, my lord, from a young lady. She said her brother—he's in the navy—had mentioned him kindly and she didn't know where else to turn. She believed she was in possession of a coded message sent from France, and enclosed it for Admiral Rafter's perusal."

"And how did she come by the note, Mr. Wilson?"

"She found it hidden in a man's clothes, my lord."

Lord Belham raised a brow, and a quirk of clear amusement appeared at the corner of his mouth. "And Admiral Rafter sends this note to me to decipher?"

The lad looked at the fearsome marquess in open astonishment. He had rarely seen him display humor when confronted with this kind of work. "Yes, my lord, as usual. Here it is."

It took only one glance for Lord Belham to recognize what was on the slip of paper, although it would take considerable work to uncover the entire import of it, and know how vital it was to British interests. Young Wilson shifted uncomfortably on his seat, his untouched brandy still clutched in his hand. The marquess stared thoughtfully across the room for a moment. "Do we know anything of the young man who was carrying this?"

"Yes, my lord. The lady sent a very complete description. He is a black-haired fellow found washed up on a beach in Argyleshire—thought to have been lost from a French ship."

To his complete horror Mr. Wilson lost his grip on the brandy glass and saw the liquor splash over his knees as the Marquess of Belham threw back his head and began to roar with laughter. "Oh, dear, sweet, beneficent heaven! And the lady's name, sir?"

"Miss Prudence Drake, my lord, but she sent no address. Is it important?"

"Oh, yes," said the marquess, recovering with visible effort. "Very important! But there is no clue to her whereabouts?"

Mr. Wilson mopped at his breeches with his pocket handkerchief in an agony of embarrassment and shook his head.

"Then," said the Marquess of Belham, rising and striding to the fireplace, "the most important thing of all now is to find out who the hell this French spy really is and track him down, don't you think?"

Chapter 8

The next day as the White Lady came into Oxford, Hal's growing suspicion became a certainty: he knew this country, he had lived here. Shipton-on-Cherwell, Kidlington, Wolvercote: the names resounded in his head like a tocsin. Over that rolling swell to the west lay the Evenlode, on the other side was the River Ray—all the bright waters running and bubbling between their green banks to swell the Isis, the upper reaches of that great flow of water known as the Thames. Hal had ridden by their banks and galloped a blood horse through these villages. He knew the interiors of the inns, and the bawdy houses, and the great houses of the local gentry. He had hunted here and fished, for both game and women. Oxford with its multitude of graceful honey-colored spires had been his home! Yet the images seemed blurred around the edges, as if he had pursued all these activities three sheets to the wind. The strain of trying to remember it all gave him a blinding headache.

It didn't help that he knew this was the end of his journey with Prudence and Bobby. What possible excuse could he make to stay with them? Prudence would send a message to her sister in Wiltshire, whose carriage would come to fetch them. Hal had done as he had promised, and delivered them both safe out of Scotland. After this the wicked marquess, his one-eyed servant, and their small quarry and his governess, were none of his business. It was a painful and heart-wrenching knowledge.

Hal closed his eyes for a moment. Dear God, the look on her face when she had finally overcome her fear of the water and begun to float! Those severe features had shone with such vivid pleasure and delight. She had laughed up at him, her small cold hand clutching his naked shoulder, and the pale silvery hair escaping from its knot to float about her head in the water; she had been free and bold and enchanting, like the Lorelei. He could still feel the place where her hand had touched his naked skin, and the place in his heart which had seemed to contract with longing as she had given him her trust. Hal had wanted with every fiber of his being to hold her wet face to his and kiss away all of her troubles and her rectitude and her doubt. So, of course, he had not done so.

Prudence had said with the clear innocence of a child, "Oh, good gracious! Hal, I'm floating! It feels like magic!"

Damnation! If he could only stay with her and bring that brightness back into her face every day! There was so much of the world he wanted to show her. Had Prudence ever been up in a balloon?—Or ridden at a gallop over the downs?—Or danced a waltz in the wee hours until she was dizzy? Hal wanted to see her face alight with joy and wonder and surprise again, and he wanted, with a desperate and unnerving passion, to see her on fire with that happiness because of him—because he had brought her to ecstasy in his bed.

The White Lady tied up at last beside docks fronted by the warehouses of Oxford, and Sam set about arranging the unloading of his cargo—the crates of teapots and cups and milk jugs they had brought from Josiah Wedgewood's potteries in Stoke-on-Trent. Sam drew Hal to one side and counted out some coins into the palm of his hand.

"Here you are then, lad. A little bonus for the sake of your new wife and the lad. She loves the boy, for all he's not hers, and that's a stroke in your favor. She'll come around, I don't doubt it. But marriage is a tricky mistress and demands her due in sadness sometimes."

With a hearty shake of the hand, Sam bid his temporary help good-bye. Prudence and Bobby similarly made their farewells to the kindly boat master and to Willie, his shy son, and to *The White Lady*, who had brought them safely from Liverpool.

With a final wave Hal shouldered their luggage and led Prudence and Bobby into Oxford.

"You seem to know where you are going!" exclaimed Prudence after a moment.

Hal stopped and grinned down at her. "Three more streets and there's an inn called the Golden Goose. You can stay there until your sister arrives."

"You know Oxford?"

"So it would seem."

Hal shifted the bags and turned about to go on up the street when the revelation came to him, complete, entire, and without question. *I know that building! And that one!* He knew the very smell of these streets and the sound of the church bells. It knocked the breath from his lungs for a moment. Dear God! Dear God! He knew who he was, and who his father was, and his brothers, and his sisters, and he knew—heaven help him— the identity of Helena!

"Is something the matter?" asked Prudence with a worried frown.

"Only that I want to ask you to marry me!" said Hal.

Prudence had released Bobby's hand and the child was running ahead of them up the street.

"What?" she said. There was an expression on his face that she couldn't decipher—as if elation and despair faced each other like fighting cocks. Hal seemed almost wild enough to be frightening.

"Now, today! Before it's too late! Marry me, sweet Prudence! 'Put off your maiden blushes; avouch the thoughts of your heart with the looks of an empress; take me by the hand and say,—Harry of England I am thine!' "

"Have you gone mad, sir?"

"We have been married once at Gretna Green! Let us marry again now, angel, in Oxford, with the blessings of English Church and law, before it's too late and the real world begins to act to prevent it."

Prudence stood looking at him, at the fine-boned features and the harebell eyes and the black hair dropping wildly over his forehead. Oh, dear God, how she loved him! She had an unexpected vision of Hal waiting for her at the altar of some ancient Norman church, and herself in a dress of cream lace— plain Prudence Drake magically transformed into a beauty, like the princess of a fairy tale. But this was some kind of madness!

He was still gazing at her with that terrifying uncertainty on his face, revealing both hope and dread. How on earth could she reply? *I love you, I would marry you even if you are a traitor to king and country, and even if you dream of another woman, and don't love me at all.*

There was a piercing scream.

Hal spun about and cursed aloud, and Prudence felt the breath stop in her throat. A man had just stepped out of an alley and grasped Bobby around the waist. The child was swung up into the air, little boots flailing against the man's brawny shoulder. Bobby screamed again.

Prudence began to run toward him, but Hal was already ahead of her, pounding up the pavement, the discarded bags scattered behind him. The man clutching Bobby gave him a wide grin.

"So there you are then, sir!" he cried. "Come home to roost in Oxford!"

The man had a long scar down one cheek, the eye covered

with an eye-patch. It distorted his face into something grotesque when he smiled. Bobby's screams had died away into great, heart-wrenching sobs of pure terror.

Hal reached into his pocket before he remembered: he had no pistol. He was unarmed and dressed like a laborer. He had no doubts at all that the man with the eye-patch was armed to the teeth and would have no compunction in dispatching him in order to seize the child. But Bobby was still squirming and kicking, and the man needed both hands to hold him. In those moments, Hal raced up to him and caught the man hard by the sleeve, thrusting him up against the wall of a building. "For God's sake!" he hissed. "Why frighten the boy?"

As the man with the eye-patch seemed to hesitate for a moment, Hal tore Bobby out of his arms and thrust him at Prudence, who had just arrived, panting, behind him. She reached frantically for Bobby, but the child slipped from her grasp to land face down in a large puddle of muddy water. The sobs became wails of indignation.

Prudence caught him up and hugged the child to her, entirely unaware of the transfer of mud from Bobby's clothes to her own.

"That bad man!" screamed the child. "That bad man!"

"It's all right, Bobby," said Hal with a deadly calm. "He won't hurt you!"

"Now, if you'll just—" began the man, still with that ugly, crooked smile.

Hal drew back his arm and hit him once, cleanly, below the jaw. The man with the eye-patch flew backwards onto the pavement and sprawled there, completely unconscious.

"Come, angel," said Hal. "Take Bobby and follow me. There may be accomplices!"

He ran back to their luggage and tossed it over his shoulder, then Prudence raced after Hal down a series of twisting alleys and into a small square. Hal ran up to a pleasant white-fronted house and hammered at the knocker.

"Pray God he's home, and doesn't have some damned starchy manservant to answer the door!"

The door opened to reveal an extremely starchy manservant who took one look at the ragged trio and began quickly to close it again. But behind him appeared the slightly bleary face of a young man with brown curls cut in the fashionable windswept, or very possibly he had just arisen from his bed and his hair wasn't yet combed.

"Good God! Harry? What can I do for you, old fellow? Have you been in a mill? Who the devil is this?"

"Wake up and have your man let us in, you stupid idiot," snapped Hal. "This is Miss Prudence Drake and the young man is Lord Dunraven. We are in need of shelter, protection, and a nice cup of tea!"

"Tea?" replied the young man. "When the devil did you start drinking tea instead of best brandy? Devil take me!"

"If you do not move your man and your own thoroughly charming, though vacant, face back into the hallway and make room for us to enter, my dear Lord Jervin, I shall give the devil personal assistance to do just that."

Lord Jervin's grin was entirely vapid, but he stepped back and gave a signal to the footman, who bowed the company inside. "Of course. Welcome to my humble abode and all that. Nice to meet you, Miss Drake, Lord Dunraven. Pray come in."

In a turmoil of emotion, Prudence followed Hal into the house.

She was soon seated in the parlor with a cup of hot tea in her hands. Hal had taken Bobby into the kitchen where the housekeeper and a gaggle of maids wrung their hands over him. He was to be bathed, given warm milk, and have his clothes changed for dry ones. Two stout footmen would guard him with their lives from any intruder. Prudence had objected that these were tasks for her, but Hal had insisted she sit down, and finally ordered her to stay in the parlor with Lord Jervin.

"For God's sake! Look at you! You're shaking like a leaf! Go and sit down in the parlor and drink up your sweet tea like the douce, well-mannered Scottish lady that you are, before you faint. Bobby will be fine. I'll have him fed and changed and tucked into a clean bed. No one can find or harm us here. Jervin is the Duke of Aberney's son.''

Beneath the humor, there had been a note of distinctly imperious rage in his voice which Prudence had felt it best to obey.

Prudence glanced up from her tea to find Lord Jervin staring at her. The considerable intelligence in his brown eyes was instantly veiled as he resumed a vacuous expression.

''You are very kind to assist us, my lord,'' she said tentatively.

How on earth did one address a duke's son who had just taken in several filthy and importunate strangers from the street? Of course, one of them wasn't a stranger. Lord Jervin obviously recognized Hal.

''Feeling more the thing, Miss Drake? Nothing like strong, sweet tea when you've had a shock! Except for brandy, of course, but my brandy's no liquor for females. Feeling quite better, are you?''

''Yes, thank you, my lord.''

''Don't suppose you'd feel like filling in a chap on the goings-on, would you? I suppose this is one of Acton's mad starts? He's had me set my footmen to guard the doors and windows, for heaven's sake! And you are most uncomfortably covered in mud.''

''Acton?'' asked Prudence. She felt suddenly faint. She was about to learn who Hal really was!

''Harry Acton, the fellow who brought you here! Oh, good Lord! You didn't know his name, did you? Have I put my foot in it? Well, I suppose it's too late now and the cat is out of the bag. How long have you been acquainted?''

Prudence began to count back to that beach in Argyle. It seemed another lifetime. She shook her head. How much would Hal want her to tell this man? What had Admiral Rafter done with that coded note she had found?

''Hal is a friend of yours, my lord?''

"Oh, yes! Old drinking cronies! Harry Acton and I go back a long way, I assure you. Both Magdalen men."

Prudence had never heard the odd English pronunciation of this Oxford college. "Maudlin men?" she asked.

"That's right."

"Then he was often foxed?"

Lord Jervin began to look a little confused. "No more than the rest of us, though we were all three sheets to the wind upon occasion, of course. But Harry can usually hold his liquor like a lord."

"Is Harry Acton a lord?" The name sounded odd on her tongue. *Harry Acton.*

"Good heavens, no! Not that his father wouldn't have liked it if Harry had been the eldest son and Lord Lenwood, instead of Richard."

Prudence was instantly lost. "I'm sorry," she said. "I don't know any of these people. Who is Lord Lenwood?"

Lord Jervin gave her a glance oddly filled with compassion. "So Harry's not owned up, then? Well, in for a penny, in for a pound. Now you know his real name, it's bound to come out. My dear Miss Drake, my disreputable friend who is now consoling little Lord Dunraven in my kitchen is the Honorable Henry Acton, second son of the Earl of Acton—family name is the same as the name of the earldom, don't you know. His older brother, Richard, is the heir and has the courtesy title Viscount Lenwood. The family's got damned great estates throughout England, so what the devil is Harry playing at now, turning up on my doorstep dressed like a navvy?"

Prudence felt as if the floor were moving under her feet— as if the exquisite Aubusson carpet might rise into the air at any moment like the magic carpet of the *Arabian Nights* and carry her off to Baghdad. Her voice seemed barely more than a whisper. "Oh, good Lord! Hal is an earl's son?"

Lord Jervin stood up and came over to her. He took the tea cup from her shaking fingers. "See here, now, Miss Drake. Buck up! It's not a disaster, you know. Perfectly respectable family, all the best connections. His mother, Lady Acton, was Lady Felicity Roseleigh before her marriage—one of the famous Roseleigh roses immortalized by Gainsborough, the beautiful daughters of the late Duke of Bydover.''

Hal's mother is a duke's daughter! Prudence gathered her courage and looked directly into his eyes. ''Is there someone in the family called Helena?''

The humor dropped from Lord Jervin's face, and Prudence caught a glimpse there of a very real discomfort. ''Oh, God! He's not over that yet, then? He told you about it, too?''

Prudence felt her heart begin to beat heavily in her breast. Was Helena a fiancée, or a sweetheart, or a wife? ''He has dreams about her! You must tell me, my lord! What is Hal— Mr. Acton—not over?''

Lord Jervin obviously struggled for a moment with his own conscience before he answered, and when it came his reply was edged with both disapproval and real concern.

''His damned unprincipled feelings, of course! He got himself completely foxed one night and told several of us he'd developed a passion for her that was driving him crazy. I was afraid for a moment that he'd blow out his brains over it. Harry met Helena at Richard's home, Acton Mead, and he's been desperately and completely in love with her ever since.''

Prudence was amazed she could still speak when it seemed that her mouth had filled with ashes. ''Why unprincipled?''

''I hear tell she's a real beauty, diamond of the first water and all that. They just got married last autumn, and it was a love match that scandalized the family. She's already expecting the next heir. Harry's in love with his sister-in-law, for God's sake! Helena is Lady Lenwood—his brother Richard's wife.''

Bobby was finally tucked up in a bed, where in spite of his protestations that it was the middle of the day and he wasn't at all tired, he fell asleep. The Honorable Henry Acton looked down at the child's sleeping face and felt the familiar stirring of love and protection at the sight of the round forehead and soft, plump cheeks. He had three younger sisters—Eleanor, Joanna, and little Milly, all older than Bobby, of course—and two brothers: golden, beautiful Richard, who had risked his life and his sanity in the fight against the French in the Peninsula, and young John who had once almost died of poison because Harry had not been smart enough to prevent it.

And Richard, the man Harry loved and admired more than any other in the world, was married to Helena. Loving, noble, beautiful Helena. Husband and wife were now deeply in love, and happy. Helena had never looked at another man since the day when Richard had ridden into her garden and asked her to marry him. She was entirely absorbed in her husband—and the child she was going to bear him in July, next heir in line to the earldom. Yet it had not been plain sailing when they were first married. Nothing in Harry's life had been more difficult than to be with Helena when his own brother had abandoned her. Harry closed his eyes, clearly remembering the pain of those feelings. Of course, he had left the country at the earliest opportunity. Harry was truly proud to know that Helena could never have guessed for one minute how he felt. And neither, thank God, had Richard.

Harry went back to the parlor to find Lord Jervin sitting there alone. The son of the Duke of Aberney looked up and flushed when his guest came in.

"Miss Drake has gone to lie down. Is the child all right?"

"He's fine. Children get over shock with enviable ease, it would seem."

"Do you want to tell me what the devil's going on, Acton?"

Harry grinned. "No, I don't. Though I'm grateful for your beneficent shelter. Suffice it to say the child has a powerful guardian who wishes to lay hands on him for possibly nefarious purposes. Until I can get to the truth of the matter, I intend to shield him and his governess, and certainly I shall prevent Lord Dunraven being snatched in the street."

Lord Jervin laughed, a little unpleasantly.

"His governess? She told me you had asked her to marry you, sir. What mad start is this? Have I interrupted an attempted seduction? Miss Drake hardly seems your usual type. And to offer marriage in order to get a respectable girl into your bed seems damned underhanded to me."

Harry went quite white and recoiled as if he'd been struck. But he met Lord Jervin's gaze until the duke's son was forced to look away. "Of course, it's the kind of behavior you believe you can expect from me, Lord Jervin?"

"Actually, no. For God's sake, Harry, I thought I knew you! I didn't think you capable of such a dishonorable action!"

Harry's voice had acquired a sarcastic bite which Prudence would hardly have recognized. "Until now? Good Lord, you don't put much faith in my character, do you? Why the hell would Prudence decide to announce to a perfect stranger that I had proposed to her? And what in God's name would make you leap to the conclusion that I would do so in order to ravish her?"

"What else was I to think after what you told me—an undying passion for your own brother's wife, for God's sake?" Lord Jervin looked defensive, but had already decided that his duty must be to protect the innocent Miss Drake, whatever his loyalty to his friend. So if Harry had dishonorable intentions, he would follow a course to thoroughly scuttle them. "Anyway, why shouldn't Miss Drake tell me?"

Harry dropped into a chair and began to laugh. "Why not, indeed?" he said at last. "But how deuced unfortunate that I chose to get so devilish foxed that night, and spill my cursed unsavory guts to my rattle-brained friends!"

Lord Jervin was looking extremely uncomfortable. He ran his hand back through his hair leaving it standing in tufts all over his head. "Is it?"

"Unfortunate enough that I am tempted to call you out, my lord. Did you see it your duty to tell Prudence?"

The duke's son was now a deep red, but to prevaricate was

not strictly lying, and it was in a deuced good cause. "Should I have done?"

"I trust not. But I might still demand satisfaction, I think. For your damned judgmental and unnecessary remarks, if for nothing else."

Jervin paled. "By God, you know I'm no match for you with a pistol, Harry! It would be murder!"

Harry flung himself back on the chaise longue and deliberately tossed his muddy, booted feet up onto the delicate brocade upholstery of the arm. "Murder? Why does that word carry so much appeal right now, I wonder? For I intend to marry Prudence Drake, whatever the world or my father may say about it, and I wish you would keep your bloody uncalled-for aspersions to yourself. But first I have to take her to Acton Mead, where my brother's heart-breakingly lovely wife will greet me with a tender kiss and tease me for being away so long. I am, after all, her dearest brother. The visit is going to be devilish uncomfortable, don't you think?"

Lord Jervin seemed bereft for a moment. "You will take Miss Drake to Acton Mead, Helena's house? Why, for God's sake?"

"Because it's the only place I can think of where she'll be safe. King's Acton is too far, and anyway, I doubt if the earl and my mother are in residence right now. Lady Acton is probably in London, in fact. I cannot leave Bobby and Prudence to the untender mercies of my father's staff. Neither can I allow her to go alone into Wiltshire to her relatives. The man we are fleeing has powerful connections. If he knows about Prudence then he knows about her family. Do you think a country squire could protect her and the child?"

"You really believe little Lord Dunraven is in mortal danger?"

Harry sat up, ignoring the mud he had left on the couch. "I don't know what to believe. It seems too fantastic, of course, but Prudence believes it and that's all that counts. So I would be very grateful, dear fellow, if instead of undermining her faith in me with your dark suspicions and gallant concern, you would lend me a carriage, some horses, and an armed guard, and help me convince Miss Drake that Acton Mead is her best hope.''

"What if I don't feel like cooperating?"

Harry stood up and looked darkly at Lord Jervin. "Then I shall slaughter you right now with the poker."

"Oh, dear God. Listen, Harry, you know I'd do anything reasonable to help you. But you can't marry some unknown Scottish governess, especially when you're nursing an unrequited love for someone else. And I'm damned if I'll stand by and let you ruin her."

"I do not intend to ruin her," said Harry with deliberate emphasis. "If that was my goal, I would have done it by now, for God's sake."

"But you can't possibly marry her! As the second son, you need to marry money and connections, don't you? Lord Acton would have a fit."

Harry pointedly ignored this exactly accurate opinion about his father. "And a change of clothes and a decent haircut and shave wouldn't come amiss. I would like to borrow your man for a barbering. Meanwhile could you send a fellow over to my old lodgings for a brace of pistols and some decent apparel? I've been living in these damnable rags since I came back from France."

"France?" queried Lord Jervin. "By God, didn't you know—Boney's back in Paris! We'll be at war again before the month's out. Why on earth did you go to France?"

A look of genuine consternation crept over Harry's face.

"Good God," he said after a moment. "I have no idea. And that is the whole and unvarnished truth, at least."

Chapter 9

"I refuse," said Prudence.

"I don't accept your refusal. If necessary I shall take Bobby to safety and bring you along in bonds behind him. Lord Belham wants only the child, but he might be prepared to hurt you in order to get to him. We are going to Acton Mead, angel, and you cannot prevent it."

Prudence looked down and bit her lip. She had surprised herself by falling asleep in one of Lord Jervin's guest bedchambers, then woken to find her bags neatly stacked at the foot of the bed and a flustered maid hovering with jugs of hot water. So she had bathed and changed, and come downstairs to find a tall, dark stranger waiting for her in the parlor.

He stood staring from the window. His hair was neatly cut and curled over his head in deep, black waves. An immaculately tailored blue superfine jacket stretched over his shoulders, and his long legs were accentuated by light beige pantaloons. As he turned and spoke, she saw that his closely shaved chin was framed by a fashionably crisp white starched collar and cravat. The Hal of *The White Lady* had disappeared. This man looked

every inch Harry Acton, son of one of the more powerful
peers in the land. Prudence was furious with herself for feeling
intimidated.

"You cannot make me, sir," she said stiffly. "Bobby is my
charge, and I shall take him to my sister as I had planned."

It still seemed to be the voice of a stranger. "Is your sister's
coachman up to snuff if it comes to a fight, Miss Drake? Do
you suppose that, after tracking you to the MacEwens and
following us to Oxford, Lord Belham's man doesn't know that
you have a sister in Wiltshire? He may even know who I am,
but that doesn't matter. We shall travel on the public turnpike
in Lord Jervin's coach with armed outriders, and my brother
Richard is the best man I know for a situation like this. I
was one of Wellington's secret scouts in the Peninsula. I doubt
that the chap with the eye-patch or any other of Lord Belham's
minions would be much use against a man who fought with
the Spanish partisans against Bonaparte. And if you remember,
I am a moderately good shot myself. With my own pistols, I
can safely guarantee you I shouldn't miss my target."

"Oh, gracious!" Prudence closed her eyes. Hal was right;
she knew it in her bones as well as with her head. If Belham
tried to kidnap Bobby again, she needed more powerful protection than her sister's household could provide. No doubt this
Lord Lenwood would know what to do. He was heir to the
Earl of Acton, with all those other powerful connections. But
his wife was the Helena of Hal's dreams, and now he had
remembered who she was, his first thought was to go to her!
Was Prudence to be witness to the destruction of a brother's
marriage as well as her own heart?

Hal looked at her white face. "And there is something else,
angel," he said gently.

Prudence glanced up at him. He seemed completely beyond
her touch, as if the very starch of his collar represented an
immovable barrier between them. Of course, the lady he loved
was of his own rank: Lady Lenwood—how would she react

when her brother-in-law turned up at her door with a governess
and her runaway charge? "What?"

He smiled, a smile of heart-breaking uncertainty, and Prudence thought she could see dread behind it. "I asked you to
marry me, you know, before we were so outrageously interrupted. I rather hoped you had considered your answer."

"Oh, I have," said Prudence, rising to her feet. He loved
his brother's wife! Miss Prudence Drake was damned if she
would take second place, and break her heart over him for the
rest of her life! And even without that, she was no match for
him, was she? A Scottish governess and the son of an English
earl! Prudence clasped her shaking hands together and willed
them to be still, but her voice broke and wavered with her
anguish. "I have considered everything about my situation very
carefully, Mr. Acton. I shall come to Acton Mead with you
because it is best for Bobby, but I will never, ever marry you."
She reached deep into some cold, dark corner of her heart
which could lend implacability to her voice, and found it. "I
say *never* because I mean it, sir. It is completely out of the
question."

Harry looked down at the carpet for a moment. He was
almost as white as his collar. "Very well," he said at last.
"I'm sorry if my offer distressed you so very much. Please
rest assured that I shan't annoy you about it. Since the thought
of spending your life with me obviously causes you so much
pain, I shan't ask you again." He glanced up at her. The
harebell eyes were as bleak as the top of Shap Fells, and seemed
fathomless in his pale face. "Let us pretend that I was never
foolish enough to ask you and put it behind us. I suppose I had
better begin readying everything for our journey, hadn't I? If
you will excuse me, Miss Drake?"

He closed the door softly behind him, leaving Prudence alone
to bite back the bitter tears that threatened to spill in a torrent
down her cheeks.

*   *   *

The carriage ride was an agony. Not physically, of course, for Lord Jervin's coach boasted the latest style in springs and had deeply upholstered seats, but because Prudence sat opposite the Honorable Henry Acton and made small talk. She knew that her Prince Hal was lost to her forever. She must henceforth think of him as Harry Acton, the earl's son, who was about to swim as far out of her life as the silkie diving into the ocean to return to his magical home in the Skerries. But there had been those golden days on *The White Lady!* For the rest of her life, whenever she was lonely and ignored as governesses must be, she had something wonderful to remember. It was an unpalatable and harsh consolation.

Harry was polite and guarded, and Prudence could tell nothing of what he was thinking. Why had she let him beguile her? Kiss her? Make her fall in love with him as if she were a green girl instead of a sensible governess? *They come to shore and marry real ladies, you know, and steal their hearts, but they always abandon them and their babies, and go back to the sea in the end.* If Harry had not stopped her that night on the narrow boat, there might even have been a child.

They traveled fast through the day, stopping only to pay tolls and change horses. No one intercepted them or seemed to be following them, but Hal sat tense and alert with his primed pistols in his pocket. It rained hard for the entire journey, and was bitterly cold. The odd early heat wave that had blessed the wanderings of *The White Lady* was over. Normal English spring had returned with its crazily unsettled weather.

By early evening they had reached the Chilterns; London was not too far ahead. Little by little their stilted conversation had tailed away. Prudence found herself watching the changing countryside in a blur of suppressed tears, while Hal—no, Harry Acton—pointed out landmarks and told enchanting stories to an excited five-year-old lord whose life was in danger. While talking to Bobby, Harry seemed untouched by her refusal of his proposal. Perhaps he was relieved! He might have found it amusing to flirt with her on the narrow boat, but now he knew who he was, he could hardly seriously consider tying himself to her for life. Thank God she had found the strength of mind to refuse him. If only it didn't hurt so very much!

It was already dark when they turned into a spacious deer park—grazed by a scattering of ghostly white sheep—and pulled up before the ivy-covered facade of an elegant small country house. Everything dripped and ran with rainwater. The ivy sparkled with a myriad of jewels in the flare of several flambeaux. A footman opened the door and another ran out to them with an umbrella. Harry leapt down from the carriage.

"Hello, Williams! Filthy night, isn't it? Can someone tell Lord Lenwood that his troublesome, scapegrace, prodigal brother has come for a visit and expects him to bring forth the best robe and the ring and the shoes, and to bring hither the fatted calf and kill it?"

"Well, bless my soul! Master Harry! Good Lord! Would you take it amiss if I were to shake you by the hand, sir?"

"Not at all." Harry laughed as the footman seized his hand and pumped it vigorously up and down. "It's damned good to see you in such hale spirits, Williams, after what happened last Christmas."

"Aye, wicked doings, sir. Wicked doings. But there's no more of that at Acton Mead these days, I'm glad to say. We're blessed with a happy household now."

Prudence ducked under a second umbrella and ushered Bobby into the hallway after Hal. A happy household? She looked about at the lovely Jacobean ceiling and sturdy old doors. It was a building of so much simple, old-fashioned, unpretentious beauty! So this calm, lovely place was Acton Mead, Helena's home!

One of the doors opened to reveal the slender figure of a woman. Her bright blond hair was dressed plainly in a knot at the back of her neck and she wore an elegantly simple gown, but her face shone like a lamp with contentment. She looked beautiful—radiating serenity and calm. As she saw the visitors she broke into a wide smile. It could only be Helena, Lady Lenwood, for her house reflected her. No wonder Harry had lost his heart! Prudence felt herself blush to the eyebrows. She tried with limited success to shrink back behind the footman as Helena came forward, hands outstretched.

"Harry! Oh, Richard will be so delighted to see you! *I'm* so delighted to see you! Where have you been? We thought you had gone off to Timbuktu and we had lost you forever. How could you not have sent word?" Helena seemed alight with pleasure.

Harry laughed and took her proffered hands. "As if I would not come back to you and my stiff-necked idiot of a brother, beloved Helena!" He smiled gaily as Helena reached up on tiptoe to kiss him. How much pain lay beneath that gallant smile?

"And who is this?" asked Helena kindly, turning to Bobby.

"Lord Dunraven, at your service, ma'am." Bobby offered his hand. "I'm quite hungry. Do you really have a fatted calf? I have always wanted to eat one."

"We shall see what we can do," replied Helena, shaking the small hand very seriously. "And if there's no fatted calf then I'm sure there are scones and honey, or maybe even chocolate cake. We'll ask Cook." Bobby beamed at her.

Then Helena held out her hand to Prudence as Harry introduced her. "Welcome to Acton Mead, Miss Drake! Any friend of Harry's is always very sincerely welcome here."

How could Helena show such a lack of curiosity or censure that her unmarried brother-in-law should turn up unannounced with an unchaperoned single lady and a child? No wonder Harry was so madly in love with her! What man wouldn't be? Helena was everything that Prudence felt she herself was not: beautiful, graceful, and entirely self-possessed.

Prudence made a small curtsy. "I am Lord Dunraven's governess, my lady."

"Well, you will be one of the family here. Acton Mead

is shamefully informal. It belonged to Richard and Harry's grandmother, you see, and they played here as boys. It's an atmosphere that none of us wants to change. Let me help you off with your wet things. You must be exhausted. How far did you come today?''

"From Oxford," said Harry. "Helena, my beautiful sister, where's Richard? I have something horrendously important to discuss with him."

"Now, isn't that typical of men!" Helena laughed. "Harry goes off to France and returns two and a half months later with no more warning than a March hare leaping from a hedgerow, and all he can think of is to discuss business with his brother." She turned to Harry with a smile full of charm. "If it's confidential, it'll have to wait, sir. We have other company, you see. Someone, in fact, who's been looking for you."

"Looking for me?" Harry raised a brow. "Not some old crony from Oxford dunning Richard for my gaming debts, I hope, because I didn't leave any. Or is it an irate father demanding I offer my sorry name to his ruined daughter and the brat she would like to pass off as mine? No, no, I can see from your attempt to frown that it's someone respectable, in which case they are pulling the wool over your eyes, dear Helena. I have no respectable connections at all."

"Except us," replied Helena. She had slipped her hand through Harry's arm and laid her head for a moment against his sleeve. "Richard and I have settled down to be the very picture of respectable, quiet domesticity. We think we deserve it after the outrages that took place at Christmas." Then she looked at Prudence and smiled again. "You must forgive me for so ignoring you, Miss Drake! Harry saved Richard's life last winter, you see, so I will always love him to distraction."

Harry turned Helena's face up to his and kissed her soundly on the forehead. He seemed filled with happiness.

"As we all love you, dear Helena! Every one of us sorry Actons worships the very hem of your skirts, even my mother and, more remarkably, my father—and not only because you carry the next heir. Acton Mead is only the haven that it is because of you, and you are the balm that daily heals Richard's soul. No, don't deny it! You are too honest to lend weight to a lie!''

Prudence shed her coat and gloves, and helped Bobby out of his. Her hands felt cold and clammy, and there was a dreadful pain in her throat as if she would never be able to swallow again.

Helena looked down and grinned as Bobby went up to her and trustingly put his small hand in hers, then she held out a welcoming arm, including Prudence in the hospitality of Acton Mead as if she were an old friend. ''Come, Miss Drake. Don't listen to Harry's nonsense. Acton Mead is gloriously old-fashioned and laid out like a maze. Let me guide you in and ring for some tea. You must warm yourself before I show you to your chamber. My husband won't mind if he meets you in your travel clothes and neither will our guest, I'm sure. And tea should come before everything else in my opinion.'' Helena looked down and smiled at Bobby. ''Tea with scones, Lord Dunraven?''

They were ushered through a series of gracious, friendly rooms, each brought alive by great vases of daffodils. At last Helena came to a sturdy oak door and laid her hand on the knob.

''Richard entertains in this little study these days. We have a grand fire in here, and it's close enough to the kitchen that the scones for Lord Dunraven will arrive still hot and dripping with melted butter. Come in!''

Helena opened the door and gestured Harry and Prudence inside. Two gentlemen were sitting in earnest conversation in front of a roaring fire. The drapes and shutters had been closed to keep out the dark of the rainy evening. A sense of warmth and security beckoned to Prudence—an ideal haven for travelers arriving on a stormy night. There was nothing overpowering or grand about Acton Mead. The room was cozy, filled with love.

A blond man stood up immediately at their entrance, and Prudence saw him exchange a glance with Helena that made her heart contract with ungenerous envy. So this was Harry's brother, Lord Lenwood. In startling contrast to the golden sheen of his hair, Richard's eyes were as black as night. There was a strong family resemblance to Harry in the straight, fine-boned nose and high cheekbones. Yet Richard seemed graver, more serious, perhaps, though contentment sat in every feature.

Helena smiled back at him. In that brief moment his eyes reflected a depth of tenderness and understanding. Was this what it meant to share love without doubt or question? Then the black eyes moved to take in the newcomers and filled with delight and laughter.

"For God's sake!" he exclaimed, striding up to them. "Harry! You're a damned reprobate, sir! Where the devil did you spring from? Do you once again promise to stay as grave and sober as a monk, and then create bedlam in my house?" Richard wrung his brother by the hand. Then the men embraced with open affection. "You must know, my lord," Richard added over his shoulder to his guest, "that the last time Harry was at Acton Mead he came in the wake of a murderer!"

Richard led Harry up to the other gentleman who had been sitting with him at the fireside. The man had risen to his feet and was looking thoughtfully at the group who had entered. Prudence judged him to be close to fifty, perhaps, though his hair was still dark. Lean and tall, he was stunningly handsome, but there was something almost sinister in the piercing eyes and strongly aquiline nose. Then he smiled at Harry and the menace in his look disappeared. Prudence shook herself. Of course Lord Lenwood's guest was not dangerous! He was just older and more powerful, perhaps, than the others, with something a little feral in his manner.

"Not this time, I trust." Harry laughed and held out his hand to the stranger. "This time I came here to avoid one."

"And the events at Christmas weren't his fault, of course, they were mine," Richard continued gaily. "Allow me to introduce Harry Acton, my lord. This is my disreputable younger brother whom you have been seeking in vain for so long." The older man shook Harry's hand. Richard grinned at them. "Harry, if you weren't such a damned shady character you could have saved Helena and myself a great deal of worry and made things a lot simpler for the marquess, though as it turns out he has done a remarkable job of tracking you down. Allow me to present his lordship, Alexander Duchain, the Marquess of Belham, who has been longing to make your acquaintance."

Prudence felt the floor move beneath her and the flames seemed to roar from the fireplace to wash over them all with unbearable heat. Yet no one else felt it. They all continued to exchange greetings like neighbors at the county ball.

"I am very pleased to locate you at last, Mr. Acton," said Lord Belham, laughing openly. "Not one of the reports I received did you justice."

"Yet I would seem to have made it so elementary for you to find me, my lord," replied Harry without any visible surprise or hesitation. "For here I am." Then he grinned with irrepressible gaiety, and with a gesture invited Prudence to step forward and join them. "And here are your small ward, Lord Dunraven, and his governess, Miss Drake. You must have felt the most dreadful anxiety about them, too."

The roar became deafening.

Prudence awoke to find herself in a shadowy chamber. She was lying on a feather bed with a blanket over her. A fire flickered in the grate and a single candle burned at the bedside.

"You are awake?" It was Helena's voice.

"What happened?" Her own voice sounded horribly feeble in her own ears.

"You fainted. I feel entirely responsible. You must have been exhausted from the journey. It was thoughtless of me to take you straight into an overheated room like that. Are you more the thing now?"

Prudence struggled up, pushing aside the cover. "I have never fainted before in my life! Lady Lenwood, I'm so sorry!"

"Please, call me Helena. And may I call you Prudence?"

"You are very kind." Prudence looked about the room and felt another flood of panic. "Where is Bobby?"

"The small Lord Dunraven? He's in the kitchen with Mrs. Hood, my housekeeper, and she is smothering him with affection, primarily in the form of baked goods. Harry is with him. My brother must be very taken with your small charge, Prudence, for he refused to leave him alone for a moment. He also said that you would want Bobby to sleep in your room tonight, so we have made up an extra bed for him, over there. Is that to your liking? For if it is not, we have a splendid nursery."

"Oh, no! Pray, let him sleep in here with me. I should much prefer it!"

"Excellent! Then we have made everyone happy. Lord Belham is very pleased to find his little ward arrived safely, as you may guess, and he wants everything arranged for Bobby as you would wish. I don't believe the marquess is terribly comfortable with small children, somehow." Helena laughed.

"Lord Belham told you he was Bobby's guardian and that he was looking for him?"

"Yes, indeed. And he knew you were traveling with Harry, so he decided to wait here for you all to arrive. But I will not tire you now with strings of silly questions. I'll leave you alone to rest, shall I?"

Helena rose to leave, but Prudence held out a restraining hand. "Lady Lenwood! Helena! Could you tell me something?"

"Of course, if I can. What did you want to know?"

Prudence swung her legs from the bed and gathered her thoughts. If she closed her eyes she could still see the string of odd symbols on that little scrap of paper. Then she looked up into Helena's face. "About Harry. Why did he go to France?"

* * *

Bobby sat at the kitchen table with his mouth full of scones and honey, the perfect image of a contented child. Harry managed to get Mrs. Hood, the housekeeper, away from Bobby's plate and to one side for a moment.

"Mrs. Hood, I know this will seem odd, but can you promise me on your most solemn oath that you won't let that little boy out of your sight for a moment? In particular, keep Lord Belham or any of his servants from being alone with the child. I want your word on it."

The rotund housekeeper glanced at the child and back up at Harry with obvious distress. "Of course, Master Harry, if you say so."

"I do say so. You remember what happened at Christmas?"

"When that wicked fellow tried to poison John and Williams? I'll never forget it, sir! Surely you don't think—"

"I don't know what to think, Mrs. Hood. But my brother John wasn't even the intended victim, and Bobby may be. He is only five years old. There's no room to take any chances, don't you see? He mustn't be left alone with anyone except myself or Miss Drake. Promise me!"

Mrs. Hood smiled across the room at Bobby. He grinned at her, but her expression when she turned back to Harry was as fierce as a broody hen's. "Either myself or Mr. Hood will stay with him every minute, Master Harry. Don't you worry. No harm will come to that little golden head in this house as long as I've breath in my body!"

Harry rejoined his brother and Lord Belham in Richard's warm study. He announced himself with an excellent joke and a charming apology for taking so long to see to poor Miss Drake and the young Lord Dunraven. He looked relaxed, carefree, and nonchalant.

"Helena has Miss Drake safely tucked up in the second-best

guest chamber. No doubt I set far too madcap a pace from Oxford, but Lord Jervin has such a deuced bang-up carriage and whenever the ostlers saw his crest they gave us the fastest prads! And of course, Miss Drake is very concerned about the child.'' Harry poured himself a brandy and crossed the room to take a chair by the fire. ''But how on earth did you know, my lord,'' he said to Belham, ''that I was escorting your run-away ward and his governess? You must have an excellent spy network!''

The marquess leaned back and stretched long legs to the fire. He was examining Harry between narrowed lashes. ''I do, as a matter of fact. But it was not good enough, of course.''

''You mean we gave your man the slip?'' Harry raised a brow and grinned with marked camaraderie, as if to be stalked across Britain by spies were an everyday occurrence.

''Several times, I regret to say. The last firm report I had of you was that you were taking part in a prize fight in Gretna Green.''

Richard laughed aloud. ''A prize fight? For pity's sake! You are truly incorrigible, Harry!''

Harry kept his attention on Belham. He didn't attempt to hide his surprise. ''Good God! Your man was there?''

Lord Belham smiled. ''He didn't witness the battle royal itself, I'm sad to say, but it was the subject of a penny sheet the next morning. You are a famous man on the borders, Mr. Acton. The only Englishman ever to have defeated Braw Jamie, I understand—a rare ox of a man and irresistible in battle.''

Richard was now almost choking with laughter, but Harry became suddenly serious and almost a little petulant.

''It was the drink defeated Braw Jamie, alas! I am no more than average with my fives, so it is not a fame fairly won. Pistols are my strength, my lord. Did you know that?''

Lord Belham idly turned the signet ring on his finger. The baleful eagles glared up at him, as if thoroughly aware of the veiled threat in Harry's words. ''But it was a fame which gave me a very complete portrait of you, fortunately, especially when added to prior descriptions gathered from your days at the Manse with Mr. and Mrs. MacEwen. It was not hard then to discover your identity from your acquaintance in London. You look very like your mother, and Lady Acton is well renowned in society, of course. As for the pistols, I would love to match you some day, sir. I am not a bad shot myself.'' He glanced back up at Harry, his black eyes glittering with some well-hidden emotion. ''When I lost track of you in Liverpool, I feared you had taken Lord Dunraven to the Americas. How the devil did you disappear so completely after that?''

Harry grinned. ''I believe I have heard some splendid doggerel to the point, my lord:

> 'Hail, fertilizing streams! Where'er ye glide,
> Reviving Commerce woos your gentle tide.
> By you rich presents every hour are sent
> To Father Thames, to Severn or to Trent.'

We came down the Grand Trunk to the Oxford Canal, Lord Belham, with a load of tea-pots. And had the best damned weather anyone could wish for. Far better than we're having now, in fact. It looks remarkably as if it's going to snow.''

There was just the smallest flash of anger from Lord Belham. He instantly covered it with an urbane lift of the brow. ''You went down the canals with a load of freight and took a small child with you?''

Harry's expression was still benign. ''Didn't you guess as much? When your man picked us up so quickly in Oxford, I was sure you had been sniffing at our heels every step of the way.''

''But I had no idea you had gone to Oxford!'' Lord Belham sat up and put down his empty glass. The simple movements vibrated with hidden power. He turned his piercing gaze again to Harry, and this time his annoyance was visible when he met that same bland smile. ''I met Richard in London and he said you'd gone missing in France, but were bound to report to him first when you came back. Which is why I came here.''

''Oh, really?'' inquired Harry. ''There was a person in Oxford I thought for sure was your man. He had an eye missing, poor fellow, and wore a patch.''

''I have no such man in my employ, sir, I assure you. I trust that my agents are discreet enough that you would not have seen any of them.''

Harry yawned, a little too obviously. ''Then I must have been mistaken. It's of no matter now, is it? Since little Lord Dunraven has safely arrived, you may get him into your clutches as soon as you like. But I wish you would tell me, my lord, why his governess saw fit to flee with him to England to start with. She seems to think that you intend Bobby some harm.''

Lord Belham rose to his feet and stared down into the fire. Each word was clipped with an anger he could no longer hide. ''A notion she was given no doubt by the Dowager Lady Dunraven, the child's grandmother. I regret to say that the lady is of unstable mind, Mr. Acton. My only concern is to see the child safe.''

''As is mine, my lord. How fortunate that we are in such close accord. Good night.'' Harry also rose and walked quickly to the door.

''It's early for you to go to bed, Harry,'' said Richard.

''Indeed, sir,'' added Lord Belham, turning from the fireplace and smiling suddenly. ''I had hoped to have a private word with you, Mr. Acton, about something quite different.''

Harry bowed and winked to his brother. ''Forgive me, my lords. It's been a long day. In fact, it's been a long month. In the morning, perhaps?''

With no visible sign of fatigue, Harry bowed again and left the room.

Chapter 10

Helena dropped onto the chair next to the bed.

"To France? Oh, heavens, it's a long story, but I suppose there's no harm in telling you. Last year my husband, Richard, uncovered an unpleasant racket," an expression of real distress passed over Helena's usually calm features, "involving young English girls being sold to France for immoral purposes. There was a house in Paris run by a Madame Relet where the girls were used. Richard found out about it when the British occupied Paris at the end of the Peninsular Campaign. We managed to uncover the perpetrator on this end and finally put a stop to the trade." Helena smiled at Prudence, who was gazing at her with blank astonishment. "In fact the man died, and Richard would have died too if Harry hadn't been there—Harry's a dead shot, you know—but there was nothing much more that Richard could do about Madame Relet. He had just come back to England after many years away, and he had a lot of responsibilities here. Not the least of which was me, I suppose, since I'm expecting our first child. After our enemy was killed Harry offered to go to Paris and do what he could to rescue the girls who were left."

"When was that?" asked Prudence. This new information seemed absurdly out-of-place. What on earth could a Paris brothel have to do with coded messages being taken to Scotland?

Helena thought for a moment. "Harry left us at King's Acton, my father-in-law's place, on the eighth of January. So he has been gone without word to his family far too long, don't you think?"

"Then all this was long before Bonaparte escaped from Elba?"

"Yes, of course. We have just heard that Napoleon was welcomed into Paris and has picked up the reins in France without opposition. The King fled immediately. Richard is most dreadfully afraid it's going to mean war again within a few months—and after all those years of death and anguish to bring about Bonaparte's defeat the first time! I pray the Corsican will surrender and not bring about more slaughter! It's too cruel!"

Helena closed her eyes for a moment, and Prudence saw in her face, along with her dread, a deep, compassionate understanding of the suffering of war. Harry had said that Richard had been a soldier, hadn't he? Was that what brought such pain to his wife's lovely features? Prudence gazed at her hands. Oh, dear heavens! Had she done the right thing with that coded message that Harry had brought from France? Had Admiral Rafter deciphered it? Whatever it turned out to be, she could never tell Helena what her husband's brother might have been involved in, because Helena so very plainly wouldn't be able to face it. But how could there be a connection between this Madame Relet and Harry's mysterious mission?

Harry checked with Mrs. Hood that Prudence and Bobby were secure in their bedroom before striding off to his own chamber. He paced about for some time, thinking over the encounter in Richard's study. Acton Mead had proved to be as safe as the lion's den. There was a certain grim irony in it. If Prudence had gone off to Wiltshire as she had planned, he could have arrived here alone and perhaps thrown the marquess off the scent. Now, what the devil was he going to do?

Harry turned and smiled at the knock on his door; as he expected, Richard stepped softly into the room. There was a faint crease of anxiety between his winged eyebrows.

"All right, Harry," he said, leaning back against the door and folding his arms across his chest. "Would you mind very much telling me what the devil is going on?"

Harry faced him perfectly seriously. "What is going on, dear brother, is that your eminent guest stands to inherit a sizable estate upon the unhappy demise of the small Lord Dunraven. His grandmother, whom one would think had no motives at all except love for the child, was concerned enough to attempt to send Bobby into hiding."

"Yes, I gathered all that. And so the child was rushed away from Dunraven Castle with his governess, who then tried to flee with him into England. Belham told me all about it. But you must have been more than your usual lunatic self to take part in such a hare-brained scheme! The child is just five, I understand. How the devil do you justify keeping him from his legal guardian?"

"I thought I had just explained."

Richard ran one hand back through his blond hair. "You expect me to believe that the Marquess of Belham is prepared to commit infanticide in order to secure title to a damp keep in the Highlands and its paltry income? For God's sake, Belham is one of the wealthiest men in the realm."

Harry flung himself back on his bed and gestured Richard into a chair opposite. "Is he? Does that preclude him from wickedness or greed?"

Richard walked to the chair and dropped into it. He met Harry's gaze without flinching. "No, of course not. But that he is respected and trusted in both society and government would seem to weigh heavily in his favor! And I believe that he has no interest at all in Scotland, apart from his mother's relatives. All of his concerns are based in London. I happen to know that Lord Belham does secret work which is vital in the struggle against Napoleon. Among other things, he has a talent for codes.''

''Well, good for him!''

''He also wants to talk privately to you about something. I suspect it is not only concern for little Bobby which brings him to Acton Mead. Belham has been tracking you down for weeks. Are you in possession of vital information of some kind?''

''Not that I know of!'' Harry's surprise turned instantly to laughter.

''So what the devil were you doing in Scotland?''

''I have no idea. 'Breathes there the man with soul so dead, / Who never to himself hath said, / This is my own, my native land!' Of course, Scotland is Walter Scott's native land, not mine. I have about as much interest in Argyle as you claim Lord Belham does.''

''You mean you won't tell me?''

Harry sat up and stared at his brother. ''I'm keeping nothing from you, Richard, I give you my solemn word. I mean, I have no idea! It would seem that I was shipwrecked in a storm— but no ship had gone missing—and that I received a blow on the head in the disaster. I suffered a very complete and grotesque amnesia. I didn't even know my own name, damn it all, until I arrived in Oxford. I have no memories of France at all. I don't even know why I went there in the first place.''

''Oh, dear God!'' Richard dropped his head in his hands and seemed to lose himself in thought for a moment. ''All right. One thing at a time. Lord Belham tells me you were found on a beach, half-drowned. Is that right?''

''The puissant marquess does have excellent information, doesn't he? Yes, I was discovered as limp as sun-bleached seaweed by Miss Prudence Drake on a beach in Argyleshire.

I was wearing a sailor's jacket and trousers over my own boots and underwear, and was as vacant and sunny as a babe.''

"Do you think someone could have knocked you over the head somewhere else and dumped you there deliberately?''

"Good God, Richard! I hadn't thought of that! You mean that there was no ship and no shipwreck at all? But Prudence heard me muttering in French, something about all being lost and abandoning ship. How would your hypothesis explain that?''

"It doesn't, of course. Very well, forget that part for a moment. Let us tackle what happened in France. You truly remember nothing?''

"All is as blank as a good footman's face, dear Richard. It's been damned unpleasant.''

"Then listen. You left England for Paris in January. I had reports that Madame Relet's brothel burned to the ground about a month later. Do you think you had a hand in that?''

"A brothel?'' Harry looked quite blank.

Richard grinned. "Oh, for God's sake! It's why you went to France in the first place.'' Quickly he gave Harry an account of the scheme involving the young English girls which they had interrupted the previous autumn. "After Helena and I were reconciled and our enemy met his death, you went to Paris to rescue some of the English girls imprisoned in the *maison*. You must have had success, since one of them wrote to me in February and gave me a very lurid and complete account of her adventures.''

"Someone wrote to you about me?''

"Little Penny from Cornwall was happily restored to her parents, thanks to the efforts of a dark-haired gentleman who had managed to gain the trust of Madame Relet. He also had very fine blue eyes and a way with him—or that's how Penny was pleased to put it. The girls escaped during a planned diversion when said gentleman set fire to the place. He had carriages waiting, and passage was already arranged to England for those who wanted it. By some miracle no one was killed in the fire, but Madame Relet was effectively ruined and has retired to Lyons. The story had your outrageous stamp on it from beginning to end. You truly don't remember?''

Harry closed his eyes and dropped his head onto his folded hands. He had dreamt of it! That confused jumble of scenes, echoing with broken snatches of rhyme and a far-off sound of screaming. *There was a young fellow who kissed / madame in her shift, but he missed* . . . A blur of gaming tables and empty wine bottles and men shouting; a building burning fiercely, its timbers crashing down in sheets of flame; the shadowy faces of women. He remembered the flames! The flames engulfing Madame Relet's brothel in Paris as he hustled the young girls, some barely more than children, into the three waiting carriages. And with a dreadful, unwelcome lucidity, everything that had happened up to that moment came back—memories crisp, unwavering, and horrific to face, as each of the disjointed images fell into place. Heavy-handed dalliance in a room hung with red velvet. The grasping hands of a woman. Flirtation which sank rapidly into carnality. Black silk sheets on a huge bed reflected in a multitude of gilt-framed mirrors. But it had been worth it for their sake—little Penny and the other girls, victims of a system as depraved and abhorrent as slavery. But, dear God, at what a price to himself!

''I am beginning to remember,'' Harry said dryly at last to Richard. ''There was tremendous confusion. I hadn't intended the fire to get out of hand so quickly—all that cheap scent and drapery was splendidly flammable, I suppose. I had been living there for a couple of weeks, laying out the escape plot for the girls.''

''For God's sake, you lived there? But how the devil did you manage to get the trust of Madame Relet? She had a deep suspicion of interfering Englishmen. She certainly saw right through me, even when I went there disguised and my hair dyed to pitch. I wasn't allowed near her *maison* after that! It's why I was so bloody ineffective in shutting the place down.''

Harry kept his head down, resting his forehead on both balled fists, but his voice was quite clear and steady. ''I managed to get inside to start with by gambling and drinking deeply enough with some other men that I met—they knew me as a Mr. Grey. I expressed a suitably prurient interest in their nasty personal habits. So they took me with them to Madame Relet's, where the innocent goods were displayed for our delectation.'' Harry flattened his hands and pressed his palms over his eyes. ''Dear God, Richard! It was bad enough to know about in theory! But to see those children paraded before us like cattle! I wanted to be sick. I kept thinking of Joanna and Milly. Some of those poor little whores were younger than our own sisters! Yet unless I fornicated with one of the girls that night, Madame Relet would have become instantly suspicious and driven me from the place without a backward glance.''

Richard's voice was very gentle. ''I do understand, my dear fellow. That is why I was never able to gain admittance again myself. So I came home to England, and did what I could with money and influence from this side of the Channel.''

''And for the girls that you did save you bought freedom from a fate worse than any of us can ever know, Richard!''

''But you lived there for long enough to put your entire scheme into action.'' There was dread apparent in every word Richard spoke, but the gentleness did not leave his voice. ''So how did you manage to allay Madame Relet's suspicions? Can you tell me?''

Harry lifted his head and gazed at his brother. His eyes were as bleak as a winter sky. There was something in his expression so haggard that Richard wanted to put his arms around his shoulders and hold him. When they were boys Richard had always tried to protect and care for Harry. But Harry was a grown man now and had chosen his own path. Richard was quite unaware that he was holding his breath in horror over what that path might have required.

''Oh, that part was easy,'' Harry replied. ''I slept with her.''

Richard's tension exploded. "Oh, my God! You damned arrogant boy!"

Harry's expression was close to a sneer. "I am twenty-four, Richard. Since I don't find cowering twelve-year-old virgins to my taste, there was no other choice, was there? Madame Relet likes pretty young men and she prefers them dark. It wasn't too revolting. In fact, you could say it was educational. She had some extremely interesting tastes, though I could just have easily have done without some of them and she is old enough to be my mother. Let us just say I did my duty like an Englishman."

"Harry, I don't know what to say. Dear God! If I had known that you would do this, I'm damned if I would have let you go!"

"You couldn't have stopped me. But the irony," the dry voice caught and broke, then recovered with an effort, "the wild, bitter irony of it all is that even as I was gaining those poor little girls their freedom by rutting with the madam, not all of them wanted to go! Some of them cursed me very soundly as the brothel burned, and told me that life as a harlot was a very great improvement over life as a farm worker or factory hand. It doesn't say much for social justice in England, does it? I felt like coming home and burning down the House of Lords, and all those damned stuffy *laisser faire* peers with it."

Richard reached out a hand, but then let it drop to his side. "Helena and I have dedicated ourselves ever since you left to trying to change the worst of those working conditions, Harry. You know that. And little Penny was grateful, believe me. I'll show you her letter. It will break your heart."

Harry stood up and shook himself. He turned to his brother with deliberate bravado. "Oh, dear God, forgive me, Richard. I've let myself get maudlin! It was the grandest adventure of my life, and Madame Relet was no worse than any other strumpet. Thank God I at last remember it! Those dreams were driving me crazy."

Richard wisely decided not to press the issue. Instead he said softly, "So what did you do in France after that, if you didn't turn up in Scotland until the beginning of March? Why didn't you come home and burn down Parliament as you intended?"

Harry shrugged. "God knows. Does it matter?"

He forced himself to try and look into the abyss. Yet after the fire there seemed to be another of those dire gaps in his memory. He could recall the flames and the girls, and the carriages carrying them safely away into the night. He had not gone with them. What the devil had he done once the brothel was gone? Why on earth would he have stayed in Paris? Furthermore, there was nothing in that appalling descent into depravity with Madame Relet which should have sent him to Scotland. Though Harry knew, of course, why he had not returned to England right away. It was the other set of images which had haunted his dreams—the rose-covered trellis here at Acton Mead, the lovely face of a woman who was oblivious to him and when they had first met sometimes downright hostile. It was the same reason he had fled England in the first place as if a bear were chasing his tail.

And to Harry's complete astonishment, Richard put the thought, quite gently, into words. "Was the reason Helena?"

Harry dropped back to the bed. "Dear God, how did you guess?"

"I'm not entirely blind, you know!" Richard leaned forward and clasped Harry's long fingers for a moment with his own. "She has no idea and I will never tell her, but I saw it in your face when you came here for Christmas. My dear Harry, I have loved you since the day you were born and Mother showed me your puce little face screaming from a lace-trimmed bonnet that had been our father's. I know you did your best to hide it, but it wasn't hard to see that your concern for Helena had become something a bit deeper than was strictly appropriate in the circumstances. Am I right?"

"As usual!" And suddenly Harry grinned and returned a

pressure full of reassurance to Richard's fingers. "But don't worry. I swear on my honor that I'm over it. You threw us together when she was very vulnerable and in need of some chivalry. But she never had eyes for anyone but you, curse your bright blond head! Of course I love her dearly and always will, but what I felt when she kissed me today in the hallway was nothing but a sweet and very appropriate brotherly affection. Helena dazzled me for a bit, that's all, and I was afraid of how I might feel if I didn't get away for awhile. But it's something completely in the past now and will stay there. Because, you see, I have fallen in love with Miss Drake. And what I feel for her is quite different from anything I ever felt for a woman before, including Helena, paragon though she is! I love Prudence enough to die for her, Richard. I have even asked her to marry me."

"Oh, dear God!" Richard groaned, but his voice was full of genuine sympathy. Then he laughed. "You might have been better to nurse an undying, chivalrous passion for my wife for the rest of your life, my dear boy. Father thought Helena an unsuitable enough addition to the family, and you are the apple of his jaundiced eye. He wants to see you wed to one of the Salisbury girls. What the hell is the Earl of Acton going to make of the marriage of the Honorable Henry Acton to a Scottish governess?"

"Don't worry," said Harry. His tone had become very remote and carefully casual. "The issue isn't going to arise. Prudence refused me. In the meantime, none of this is going anywhere toward solving the present crisis, which is what the hell are we going to do about little Lord Dunraven and his wicked guardian?"

Richard sat back. A weight of concern had been lifted from his mind, only to be replaced with a new one. When he had abandoned Helena the previous October after less than a month of marriage, it had been for compelling enough reasons—his presence seemed to be putting her life in danger. But he had not had any idea that by asking Harry to keep an eye on her,

he would impose an almost intolerable burden on his brother.
He had seen it when things had all come to a head at Christmas:
Harry fighting his inappropriate feelings for Helena, and hiding
them behind banter and nonsense. Yet it was Harry who had
moved heaven and earth to help save his brother's marriage
and his brother's life, even in the face of Helena's mistrust.
Richard closed his eyes and savored the depth of his love and
respect for Harry. He didn't deserve such a brother, any more
than he felt he had ever deserved Helena. And so now he must
show him the courtesy to take his concerns about Lord Belham
seriously, whatever his own judgment in the matter.

"What, other than the fears of Miss Drake, leads you to
believe that Belham is a villain, Harry?"

"Simple. He denied any knowledge of the man with the
eye-patch. I didn't make that up, you know. The man was
asking after Prudence and Bobby in Argyle. It was why she
fled. Then he was on our heels all the way down through
England. I saw him myself in Carlisle. If you need any more
proof, he managed to snatch Bobby in the street in Oxford,
and would have escaped with the child if I hadn't knocked
him down. I don't trust the marquess, Richard, and the risks
are too great. Think how you would feel if any harm befell
that child under this roof!"

Richard stared thoughtfully at the fire. "Of course it can't
be risked, I do see that. But Belham has been my guest here
for several days. Indeed, I thoroughly like him—he's a man
of very real intelligence and sensibility. If he's planning to
murder a child, then he's a damned fine actor. But in law
Belham's control of Lord Dunraven is absolute. What would
you like to do?"

Harry grinned. "I wrote to Mother from Oxford. She is the
only person I know who has the power to stand up to a marquess.
My plan was to wait here for her to arrive from London and
see if I could persuade her to take Lady Dunraven's side. Surely
grounds could be found to have the guardianship changed?"

"So our lovely mother is about to arrive at Acton Mead!

For God's sake, Harry! We'll have hysterics among the staff at the presence of so many of the *beau monde* at once. Of course, Mother will be delighted to see you, she might even lend her weight to your cause with Miss Drake. You know, beneath all that sophistication and elegance I have begun to believe that the exquisite Lady Acton is a romantic at heart.''

Harry swung from the bed and strode across to the fireplace. He began to attack the fire with the poker. It revealed a swordsman's grip and deadly thrust that were entirely wasted on the innocent coals. ''For God's sake! The last thing I want is to enlist Mother to help me marry Prudence!''

Richard's eyes narrowed slightly. ''My dear boy, I thought you were in love with her.''

''I am. There will never be anyone else as long as I live.'' Harry violently tossed down the poker and it crashed into the fire irons, sending metal tongs and shovels to the floor in a cacophony of noise. He strode away across the room and turned wildly to face his brother. ''But do you think—after what I told you about Madame Relet—that someone like me should marry someone like Prudence Drake? It's grotesque. It would be as if the gargoyle off the church roof were to come down and proposition the Madonna.''

Richard looked up, his black eyes like pools. ''Harry, my dear boy!'' Then he dropped his golden head into his hands. His voice when he spoke seemed filled with despair. ''So will you at least stay here until Mother arrives?''

''I don't know,'' replied Harry stiffly. ''That's rather up to Prudence.''

Prudence lay in the shadowed bedroom and listened to Bobby's light, even breathing as she stared at the ceiling. Harry had led her straight into disaster! They were trapped at Acton Mead. In spite of all the good intentions of Helena and Richard and their household, Lord Belham would only need a few minutes alone with Bobby for an accident to happen. A curious child climbing into the stall of a nervous horse, or tumbling into a ditch or a pond, and Dunraven Castle would be part of the Belham estates.

But how were they to escape, and where were they to go? Acton Mead seemed to lie in extensive grounds in a fold of small hills. To get to the nearest village would be a considerable walk, and to the nearest town with a stage coach? It was unthinkable when the journey had to be made with a small child and the weather had turned so treacherously cold and wet. Furthermore, Prudence had no money. Yet she knew that she could not stay here, waiting and watching until the axe should fall.

She slipped from her bed and crossed the room to gaze down at Bobby. He slept with one small hand curled against his chubby cheek. The fine, fair hair shone like silver on the pillow. There was no way to save him, was there, except to beg Harry's help once again? Prudence closed her eyes for a moment. Harry had asked her to marry him! Whatever had made him do it? But she would not give in to her own desire when it was beautiful Helena who appeared in his dreams.

Prudence went back to the bed and pulled on her dressing gown. The fire had burned down and the room was cooling. What an appalling treachery to fall in love with your own brother's wife! Yet who was she to say that Cupid should choose only appropriate targets? For plain Miss Prudence Drake was in love with the Honorable Henry Acton, and it was the greatest folly of her life! Only for Bobby's sake, would she go to Harry now and ask his help. And for Bobby's sake, she would crush her own feelings as ruthlessly as she was able.

Before she should lose her nerve, Prudence went to the door. She knew which was Harry's room, because she had asked Helena about it. Helena had not even raised an eyebrow at this improper request. No doubt she thought that Harry and Prudence were lovers. After all, they had traveled together unchaperoned, and Prudence had stayed with Harry in Lord Jervin's bachelor apartments in Oxford for a night with no other lady in the house. In the eyes of the world, she was already a ruined woman, wasn't she?

Prudence crept down the silent hallway and sent up a small prayer as she knocked softly, turned the knob, and stepped into Harry's bedroom.

Chapter 11

"Is this a visitation from heaven, angel, or am I about to receive an angry denunciation of my folly in bringing you and Bobby here to Acton Mead? I admit it was foolhardy as things turned out, so berate away if you wish."

Harry lay still dressed in his shirtsleeves and pantaloons on the bed, a candle burning brightly on the table beside him. He had his hands crossed behind his dark head, and he seemed to be admiring the intricate plaster work of the ceiling. Beside the candlestick stood a bottle and a half-filled glass. The brandy glowed softly in the flickering light of the little flame.

Prudence took a deep breath. "I'm not angry. There's no use at all in regrets!"

Harry turned and propped his head on one elbow. There was something in his eyes that Prudence had never seen there before—something so wild it almost frightened her. Oh, dear God! Was this the result of seeing Helena again?

"Speak for yourself, angel! Allow me all the damned regrets that I want."

"Oh, Hal! Please don't! Are you foxed?"

Harry rolled back and flung out his arms in a wide gesture, then he closed his eyes and lay in silence for a moment. When he spoke, his voice was gentle. "A little, maybe. I'm sorry. It doesn't matter. What can I do for you, Miss Drake?"

"Bobby must get away from here and I cannot take him without your help!"

"Ah. So you think we should once again take to the road in the dark of night? Shall we tiptoe to the stables and harness Richard's curricle? There will be grooms who will know we are doing it, but I'll buy their silence until morning, and Richard has probably already given them a quiet word not to interfere with anything I want to do. Shall we sneak away from my brother and from Helena, and from the warm welcome of Acton Mead—like villains?"

"We only need hide somewhere safe while I send word to the dowager. Lady Dunraven must have some plan for her grandson."

"Very well, angel. Then we shall go straight to London to the rooms of a friend of mine, Leander Campbell, and meet my mother there."

Prudence sat down as if her legs were candles wilting in the heat of a fire. "Your mother?" she said faintly.

Harry sat up. "I wrote to her from Oxford. Lady Acton is a formidable force in society. I have every faith that her influence and connections will be enough to discover a perfect solution to Bobby's problem. She was a duke's daughter and hasn't forgotten it. So what do you think?"

"Lord Belham will come after us as soon as he knows we have gone, won't he?"

"We shall have eight hours lead on him. He'll never find us at Campbell's place, and now that he's here and thinks we are trapped, he'll be less on his guard, won't he?"

"Thank you," said Prudence. "I can be packed and have Bobby ready in half an hour. But how shall we get out of the house without being seen by the footmen? Suppose Lord Belham has bribed one of them?"

"Why, I shall go down the ivy with the luggage, of course, as Richard and I did as children, and open the back door for you. If anyone sees you, say you are taking Bobby to the kitchen for some milk. Of course, there are two drawbacks to this whole splendid plan."

"Which are?"

"Firstly, that I'm going to feel like a damned fool if Lord Belham turns out not to be a villain, after all."

Prudence shrugged, eloquently dismissing this. "And what is the second problem?"

The candlelight shadowed Harry's features, exaggerating the beauty of brow, cheekbone and chin, and the sardonic lift to the corner of his mouth. "That you are sitting on my bed in your nightgown, a vision of innocence and allure, and I'm trying to decide what the devil to do about it."

Prudence leapt up and pulled her dressing gown about her body with both hands. "I did not mean any invitation by coming here like this and you know it."

Harry spun from the bed and caught her by the wrist, then forced her back until she was trapped with her back against one of the tall posts. "Did you not, Prudence? But what if I am more than a little foxed? Can you trust me if I am befuddled and sodden? What if I am three sheets to the wind? What if I have remembered what I truly am? And supposing it is not noble or virtuous or gentlemanly? Perhaps I am the kind of rogue to take advantage of a lady, after all?"

She gazed up at him, willing her heart to slow down. The faint, sweet smell of brandy brushed over her cheek. The grip of his fingers burned into her skin. "What do you mean?"

Harry released her wrist, but only to take her dressing gown in both hands and peel it back from her shoulders. The lowered sleeves pinned her arms against her sides. "You told me once that if I had murdered someone I would know it in my bones. You said I would feel the enormity of it every day weighing down my soul. Don't you remember?"

She looked up into his troubled gaze—the deep blue of

harebells, or cornflowers, or a Highland sky in the mysterious never-night of midsummer. "I don't understand. What have you remembered?"

Harry's fingers slowly moved up her arms in a luxurious, lazy caress. He began to untie the strings at the neck of her nightgown. She felt his smooth nails and fingertips brush tenderly against the sensitive skin of her throat. Prudence closed her eyes. She was shaking. His exquisite touch was dissolving all of her defenses. She loved him! Did it matter that he didn't love her? If it would somehow help him in this unknown anguish to use her, she would let it happen, wouldn't she?

Harry peeled open the white muslin to reveal the soft skin of her neck and throat. With both hands he began to push the fabric aside until her shoulders lay naked under his cupped palms, leaving her nightgown bunched over the swell of her breasts. To her shame Prudence longed for him to touch them. But his fingers ran over her bare skin to trace her collarbone and the curve of her neck. With a long, sure stroke he ran his hands up under her hair, over and over again, trailing delicate, exquisite fire from the tips of his fingers into the depths of her soul. She wanted him to kiss her. She wanted to kiss him back—to kiss away all of his strangeness and sorrow, to rediscover the lighthearted Hal of *The White Lady*. But with both hands buried in her hair, Harry dropped his head against her shoulder, so that his soft, black hair brushed her chin, and stood there, silent. Prudence shrugged out of her dressing gown so that she could move her arms. Without hesitation she took his head in both hands and held him against her breast, stroking the dark waves. The pounding of her heart must surely deafen him?

"I have killed a man," he said. There was undiluted agony in the words.

"Oh, dear heavens! Hal, please!" She was lost, bereft of all compass and direction, and only knew she was crying when she felt her own tears fall scalding onto the backs of her hands.

Harry lifted his head and looked down at her. There was nothing that could explain the pain and hunger Prudence saw in his eyes. But suddenly he smiled with some deep and desperate mockery. "His name was Harry Acton. I have killed my own soul, angel. And who will forgive me the enormity of *that?*"

Prudence said nothing. A torrent of pain had stolen her tongue and left her mute and helpless in his arms. But suddenly Harry laughed. He caught the neck of her night rail to bring it together and tie it at the neck. She could feel his fingers tremble a little against her throat. "By God, I think I am devilish drunk, after all! Leave my bedroom, Miss Drake, before it's too late—and pray forgive this maudlin scene. Do I frighten you?"

Prudence shook her head.

Harry caught her to him for a moment and dropped a kiss on the top of her head. "Brave Miss Drake! Give me half an hour to swill some coffee. By then I trust I shall not be too damned foxed to drive. Once I deliver you safely to my mother I'll leave this cursed country, so you won't be subjected to any more of my odd starts. Will that do? Take Bobby out through the kitchen door. I'll meet you there."

With a strange, painfully rueful grin he released her and strode away to the fireplace. Prudence caught up her gown and shrugged into it before hurrying away to her room where she could face each bleak, desperate emotion and attempt to destroy it. For she knew that she loved him with the same utter desolation and hopelessness that she had felt from the beginning. That she could neither reach him, nor help him, was as bitter as gall.

It was raining hard, pounding on the trees in the deer park, churning the driveway to mud. The light carriage splashed through the downpour and turned out of the gates of Acton Mead toward London. Prudence hugged Bobby to her side as Harry tooled the team around the worst of the puddles. He seemed to be completely sober, and had said not a word about that extraordinary scene in his room. But the mystery surrounding Hal had become as deep and as black to Prudence as the forbidding darkness that enveloped them. Bobby stirred against her skirt and she laid her hand over the child's back. Then she leaned her head back, closing her eyes to shut out her despair.

An explosion of sound shattered the night. She must have drowsed for a moment! Their carriage had jerked to a stop.

"My apologies for firing, sir," said an unknown voice. "Devilish rude. But it was necessary to get your attention, for I believe you intended to drive right past us? Pray, don't shoot back, I beg of you. We have you completely surrounded."

Prudence sat up and peered into the darkness. Their way ahead was blocked by a large closed carriage turned across the road, the lamps shining dully through the rain. Four horses were shifting and blowing nervously as the downpour battered at them. Harry's pair tossed their heads in sympathy, ears flat, making the harness jingle. Prudence looked about. Oh, dear heavens! What other choice had there been but to stop? Immediately in front of them was the man who had spoken, mounted on a tall bay. On each side of the curricle sat another horseman with a drawn pistol. They were all muffled in leather hats and loose cloaks. They all had handkerchiefs tied over their faces.

"Oh, for God's sake," replied Harry. His voice expressed a mild exasperation with an underlying hint of amused indifference. "The high toby lay—highwaymen? You will forgive my impatience, gentlemen. I am in somewhat of a hurry. Here is my purse! Pray drink my health with the contents."

Harry reached into his coat pocket. In one rapid movement he pulled out a pistol, took aim toward the carriage, and fired. There was a spurt of flame and an explosion of smoke, but no ball sped from the barrel. The Acton Mead horses jerked forward and Harry had to use both hands to steady them. And suddenly he was laughing with a genuine spurt of hilarity.

"Alas," said the first voice with a little more menace. "Your pistol appears to have flashed in the pan. Whereas my pieces, as I have already demonstrated, are in prime working order. Did you mean to kill me, sir?''

''I am a better shot than that,'' said Harry dryly. ''I meant to wing your coach driver, causing him to lose control of the team. The horses would have startled and cleared the road for me. Instead, now you clearly have the advantage of me, sir, and will leave considerably richer from tonight's adventure than I would have wished. You may have my purse, after all.''

''Can I trust you to deliver it? Perhaps, in the meantime, you would kindly step from your carriage?'' The horseman gestured with his pistol.

Harry hesitated for a moment as if considering whether to attempt to reach his other pocket.

''For heaven's sake,'' whispered Prudence. ''Let them have our gold! Pray, don't try to fire again when a return ball might harm the child. What is a little money against the risk?''

''But we don't know what we risk, angel,'' replied Harry softly. ''Yet I don't believe these men intend harm to you or Bobby—they have made no move to seize him. Stay here.''

Harry tossed aside his useless pistol, swung down from the carriage, and stood bareheaded in the rain. The horseman who had spoken gestured to the others and they rode up on each side of him.

''I'll have his greatcoat,'' said the highwayman grimly. ''For there is no doubt a mate to that pistol in his other pocket.''

Harry shrugged out of his coat before the men could touch him and tossed it onto the road. ''Perhaps you would like my shirt and waistcoat, too, sir—or my boots? Damned cold night to strip, but they say that mud is a wonderful conditioner for the complexion and rainwater the purest shower one can take.''

One of the men leaned from his saddle to hook Harry's coat with his riding crop and feel in the pocket. He thrust the weapon that he found there into his saddle bag.

The highwayman's pistol barrel still remained unwavering, pointed at Harry's heart. ''So does our pretty young cove have another pistol in his boot? Or a knife, perhaps?'' He grinned unpleasantly. "No, keep your boots on for now, sir. But pray leave your hands where I can see them."

Harry raised his hands and spread out his arms in a wildly insulting gesture of defiance. The rain beat over him, soaking his clothing and causing the thin fabric of his shirt sleeves to cling to the lean, strong muscling of his arms and shoulders. Another of the men instantly took aim at Harry's heart. Did he want to die at the hands of these ruffians?

Prudence pulled out the little purse of gold that Harry had given to her and held it out. "Here, sirs! This is all of our money! Pray, take it and be gone!"

They ignored her.

"A very fetching insolence, sir! So you have not learned your lesson, even now, when we have you at our mercy and I am kind enough to let you keep on your blasted boots." The highwayman circled his horse and glared down at Harry. "Such confidence ill becomes an unarmed man standing helpless in the mire. If your weapon had not misfired I might be a dead man now, in spite of your pretty tale of startling the horses. I believe I owe you a little something for that, you damned, arrogant popinjay!"

Before anyone else could react the man spurred his horse, swung his pistol by the barrel, and with sickening force brought the stock down on the back of Harry's skull. Harry dropped to his knees in the mud and grasped at his head with both hands. He did not make a sound. Prudence bit back her scream and turned Bobby's face into her own body, holding him tightly against her. The child was sobbing quietly.

"Here, now!" shouted a new voice. "None of that! He's not to be harmed!"

A man leapt from the coach and ran over to the little group. His big leather hat entirely shielded his face as he leant over Harry. "Here, Mr. Acton," said the newcomer, not unkindly. "Just come along quietly now, and there'll be no more of that."

"I trust not," replied Harry. His voice was thick, but there was still that irresistible flash of humor. "For what is the fun of beating a corpse? My head might be dense, sirs, but it is unfortunately no match for cold, hard steel. Another blow like that and you will have to search for me in Hades if you want to offer further punishment.''

The man took Harry's arm to pull him to his feet. Harry swayed against him, rain running over the planes of his face and plastering his hair to his head. In one place the water seemed to run darker and was soaking a black stain into Harry's collar. Prudence knew it was blood. Please, God! Don't let him be seriously hurt! Please, God. Let it be a ruse, she thought wildly. Harry will knock them all down as surely as he knocked out Braw Jamie, and we'll escape!

But Harry staggered as the man held him steadily upright. ''If you've cracked his bloody skull, it's the devil himself will take revenge,'' he shouted at the highwayman. ''You weren't hired for murder!'' The man slipped his sturdy arm about Harry's waist. ''Come, lad. Come into the carriage. I'll see to that head myself. A fellow as stubborn as you will be harder to kill than that, I imagine.''

The man helped Harry walk toward the closed carriage and handed him up the step. Prudence watched with a torment of emotion as Harry collapsed onto the seat, his head still gripped in both hands and blood welling between his long, elegant fingers. The man who had rescued him turned to speak again to the highwayman. Prudence couldn't hear what he said, but in the light from the coach lamps she saw his face for the first time. In a scene out of a nightmare, helplessly she reached out a hand. But Bobby sat sobbing into her coat, his small fingers clutching at her and his fragile body shaking with fear. She could not abandon the child, not even for the love of her life. And what could one woman do against four men armed to the teeth?

The door of the carriage slammed shut and the coachman whipped up the team. The carriage holding Harry and the man who had saved him lurched about and disappeared into the darkness. As they left, the highwayman who had first spoken rode over to the light curricle and pulled out a blade. He leant from his horse and slashed at the traces, freeing Prudence's team, so that her horses also galloped away into the night. In the next instant the three highwaymen had followed them.

Miss Prudence Drake and little Lord Dunraven were alone in their curricle on the King's high road, while the rain roared down from an unrelenting heaven. Prudence squeezed her eyes shut and took a deep breath. She must be strong, for Bobby's sake. But Harry had been kidnapped by a man with a great scar slashing over his features: a man with an eye-patch.

"Good heavens! Would you like salts, my dear? Nub, pray bring my salts!"

Prudence opened her eyes. A woman's face was peering in at her. It was a very beautiful face, fine-boned, exquisitely expressive. Both hair and eyes were jet black, which only set off the perfection of the lady's complexion. It took Prudence several minutes to notice the very tiny, fine wrinkles at the corners of the lady's eyes, and the amused, mature cynicism of her expression beneath the extremely fashionable little hat and veil. The sun was shining. It was morning.

"You have been set upon, I must suppose," continued the lady, "by highwaymen? And they even took your horses? It is really a disgrace in this day and age—and so close to Acton Mead. I shall have to speak to my son about it."

"Your son?" asked Prudence, but she already knew the answer. The family resemblance was too strong to miss.

The lady smiled. "Lord Lenwood. Acton Mead is his home; it's not far. I believe I shall have to take you there. I am the Countess of Acton, my dear. Lord Lenwood is my eldest son."

"Oh, gracious!" To her dismay, Prudence burst into tears. "If we had only waited, you would have arrived in time, and Hal—Harry—wouldn't have been kidnapped! Oh, Lady Acton, we've been such fools, and it's all my fault!"

* * *

Harry woke up to find his arms very thoroughly bound behind his back and his head throbbing like the very devil. He opened one eye and looked about. He was lying on the seat of a coach opposite the man with the eye-patch. The coach appeared to be traveling at some speed for he was being shaken like meal in a sieve. Harry was very much afraid that if he was shaken much longer, he would—like the wheat—simply fly apart into floury dust. He closed his eyes again and swallowed hard.

"So how did you lose it?" he asked.

"Then you're awake, Mr. Acton?" replied the man. "Is there still much pain, sir?"

"Enough," said Harry dryly. "But you must know something about pain yourself, sir. Was your eye lost in battle, or is it just the result of some piece of villainy?"

The man touched one hand to his face and made a small grimace. "Badajoz, sir. It don't hurt now."

Harry braced his feet against the rolling of the coach. "Villainy enough, then. I was not in the Peninsula, but my brother was. He has told me enough. A French saber cut, I presume?"

"I had my revenge, Mr. Acton. Pulled the frog from his horse and skewered him with my bayonet before I passed out myself. I was a sergeant, sir. Sergeant Keen, at your service."

Harry grinned. "Then, sir, with your *keen* appreciation for the exquisite aftermath of an injury to the head, I wonder if you might untie this rope? I am a mite uncomfortable, sir."

Sergeant Keen fixed Harry with his one good eye. He was not smiling. "I've already felt the force of your fist! You'll not try to bolt, Mr. Acton?"

"I'll give you my parole, Keen. I shall consider myself your prisoner and the consequences be damned. You have my word that I shall not try to escape—at least today. Therefore it would be an act of considerable mercy if I could be allowed the use of my hands."

Sergeant Keen pulled a small knife from his pocket and cut the ropes which bound Harry's wrists.

Harry sat up and dropped his head to his knees for a moment. "I believe, sir, that it might be advisable to stop the coach for a moment."

"You have given your word!"

"Indeed. And I'll keep it. But for God's sake, man, I believe I'm about to cast up my accounts."

Keen rapped on the panel and the coach swayed to a stop. Harry looked up at him and grinned. His face was as white as his cravat.

"Damn those rat-tailed fellows!" spat Sergeant Keen. "I had to hire them to help, for I knew I'd never nab you alone, but I'm sorry the cove struck you. Crack to the nob make you sick, then?"

"No," said Harry with a wry grin. "It is the things I have recalled, sir, which are raising my bile. Your friend's blow to my skull seems to have restored the rest of my errant memory. Events are beginning to fall into a pattern which is delightful in its symmetry. I have just remembered a French gunsmith and an importunate message from Scotland. Furthermore, I now also recall that I brought a paper with me from France which no doubt your employer will be most anxious to secure."

The man with the eye-patch grinned. "Aye, Mr. Acton. We'd all like to see the paper, sir."

Harry sighed. "Yet only the devil knows what has become of it. Thus I now know where you are taking me and I believe I shall not receive a very warm welcome. Isn't that cause enough for a little nausea, Sergeant Keen?"

Chapter 12

Prudence stared into a roaring fire, facing Richard and his mother, Lady Acton. She was holding a large cup of hot chocolate in both hands. Helena sat beside her on the chaise longue, a hand laid comfortingly on her knee. Bobby had been put back to bed and Mrs. Hood was sitting with him. The housekeeper had sworn on her mother's grave, the soul of her grandfather, and her apron strings that she would not leave the boy alone.

"Why must my children always involve themselves in such desperate coils?" asked Lady Acton. "Richard, I pray you will tell me who would want to kidnap Harry."

"Alas, he did not tell me, madam." Richard leaned forward as he fixed his black eyes on Prudence. He looked very grave, his winged eyebrows drawn together. "There is no doubt that these men wished to capture my brother personally?"

"None at all," said Prudence. "The man with the eye-patch called him by name. I'm sorry, Lord Lenwood. We thought that it was Bobby who was in danger."

"Bobby?" Lady Acton fluttered her fan. "Oh, you mean

the child, little Lord Dunraven. Why would the boy be in peril?''

Prudence blushed and looked down at her lap. ''His grand-mother, Lady Dunraven, believes Lord Belham intends Bobby harm. She made me take him into hiding. I'm sorry, my lord,'' she glanced nervously up at Richard, ''since the marquess is your guest. But if Bobby dies, Lord Belham inherits every-thing.''

''So Harry informed me.'' Richard stood up and stretched. ''Oh, dear God, why the devil did Harry go to Scotland instead of coming home? And what the hell else was he doing in France?''

Prudence studied the ring of anxious faces. These people were Hal's family. They loved him. Surely now she owed them the truth? ''He brought a message,'' she said. ''It was in code.''

Richard spun about. ''What?''

''I found it hidden in his jacket.''

''And what did my son do when you showed him this mysteri-ous missive?'' Lady Acton sighed and fluttered her fan again. ''I begin to think it impossible that I shall ever enjoy a peaceful old age surrounded by my grandchildren, when my sons are so very careless of their safety.''

Prudence swallowed. Lady Acton might sound flippant, but her fear was obvious beneath it. ''I did not show it to him. He didn't know who he was and I had no way of knowing what kind of a person he might really be. I thought the note might have been treasonous. I sent it to Admiral Rafter in London.''

''In which case,'' said Richard with a wry smile. ''He would have given it to a certain lord who has a gift with codes. And since that gentleman is in this house at this moment, what better than to ask him?''

Helena looked up at his face. ''Surely you don't mean—''

''But I do, love.'' Richard moved to stand by Helena. He laid a hand on her shoulder in a gesture of unconscious tender-ness. ''It is time, I believe, to consult Lord Belham about my wayward brother.''

"Then, pray, invite the marquess to join us, Richard." Lady Acton stood up as the fan snapped closed in her hands. "I am most uncomfortable at the thought of Harry in the hands of ruffians, particularly when Miss Drake tells us that they gave him a severe blow to the head. Harry may be as stubborn as a mule, but I don't believe that he has an ass's skull. Thus, distasteful as it may be to involve him, it would seem that we must put Harry's fate in the hands of Black Belham."

Prudence dropped her cup, then blushed scarlet as chocolate spread over the carpet.

"Don't worry," said Helena warmly. "The carpets at Acton Mead are used to it."

Harry touched his hand to his head. The carriage was once again racing north, causing the seats to rock like ships at sea. Sergeant Keen appeared to have given him a very neat bandage. There was no question that he was indeed an old soldier. Harry leaned back and kicked his feet up on the opposite seat. Apart from a screaming headache and the remaining unpleasant curl of nausea, he seemed to be uninjured. Beneath the pounding hammers in his skull, Harry's thoughts and memories rang clear as a bell. He tried his best to make sense of them.

"Tell me, sir," he said idly after a moment. "Why did you seize the child in Oxford?"

"Little Lord Dunraven? Why, the lad ran straight into me, Mr. Acton. I meant him no harm, I assure you. No, you're the one as I've been paid and contracted to trace and bring back, sir. And a merry dance you've led me!"

Harry glanced from the window at the passing fields and trees. It was raining again. He laughed. "I seem to have led everyone a merry dance, including myself. But if we can't dance and be merry, then life is a short, sorry mess, isn't it?"

Sergeant Keen looked at his prisoner with undisguised curiosity. "Now why the devil should a young cove like you be so bitter about life, sir?"

* * *

In the small study at Acton Mead, the fire was dying down. Every possible explanation and idea had been exchanged.

"Then I think," said Lord Belham at last, "that we should go to Scotland at the earliest opportunity."

Lady Acton laughed at him over her fan, but there was a brittle edge to her voice. "You are prepared to leave the delights of town to rescue my son, Marquess? I am so grateful that I believe I shall also journey to Scotland. Someone must act chaperone to Miss Drake, after all." She turned to Prudence. "I believe you should come, Miss Drake."

"Why?" said Prudence. Her heart was beating too hard again.

"You are the only one here who can recognize Harry's attacker, my dear. You will escort us, too, Richard?"

"Of course, madam," replied Richard. "Harry saved my life last winter. I owe him that much at least." His eyes met Helena's. She smiled at him.

"I cannot leave Bobby," said Prudence. "And he cannot travel so far again!"

"Bobby can stay with me." Helena took Prudence's hand and squeezed it gently. "No harm will come to him here, Miss Drake. I promise you."

Lord Belham studied her gravely. His expression held something that Prudence couldn't understand, something which still caused a small curl of uneasiness. "If you will grace us with your company, Miss Drake, I shall endeavor to convince you while we travel that I am not responsible for Mr. Acton's abduction—although I admit I would like to talk to him. Neither do I intend harm to the small Lord Dunraven, in spite of everything the dowager countess may have told you." The marquess held up his signet ring. He smiled, but it held a grim enough edge. "These baleful eagles have haunted me all of my life. It is the very devil to have such a splendid reputation for wickedness, but in this instance I must ask you to trust me, Miss Drake.''

Prudence hesitated. How could she know whom to trust?

Lady Acton stood up and her black gaze met Lord Belham's. Every line of the countess's elegant figure was rigid, like that of a horse suddenly scenting danger and throwing up its head. She did not turn away from the marquess, although her words were directed at Prudence. ''I can guarantee that the child will be safe at Acton Mead. After all, his wicked guardian will be on the road to Scotland and getting further from the boy every day. But I cannot be certain of the safety of my son.'' She seemed to be truly apprehensive. Oh, Lord, thought Prudence, if Lady Acton is afraid! ''Surely you would not refuse us your assistance, Miss Drake?''

Prudence looked away from her and caught Helena's reassuring smile again. She closed her eyes for a moment. There were undercurrents in this room she couldn't possibly understand—which of them were a danger to Harry? Bobby had surely earned a respite from travel and change. Helena would give him all the warmth and love that anyone could wish. And this time, she must put Harry before the child, for whatever the mystery about him, plain Miss Prudence Drake had become part of the puzzle. If Fate would somehow grant her that chance, she would sacrifice anything to be part of the solution.

''If I can be of help, I will gladly come with you, my lady,'' said Prudence. ''But only because I trust Lady Lenwood with Bobby more than it seems I can trust myself. With me he has been in discomfort and danger for weeks.''

''Then, for heaven's sake, let us call for the carriages! We shall put ourselves in Lord Belham's hands—since he seems to know more about Harry's purposes than his own family—and see how far we can trust him.'' Lady Acton gave the marquess a dazzling smile. He did not smile back. Instead he fixed her lovely face with his dark gaze until she turned away. A small flush colored her perfect complexion and she closed her fan with a snap.

* * *

It was a very different journey from the wild flight Prudence had made south with Hal: two expensive carriages, each emblazoned with a coat of arms; a bevy of outriders arranging their team changes and accommodation ahead as they traveled; the most direct route on the main turnpike north. Richard rode with the marquess in his great coach with the glaring eagles on the door panel. Prudence traveled with Lady Acton and tried to avoid Lord Belham. How could she trust him? He had admitted that Harry's coded note had come to him from Admiral Rafter and that he knew what it meant. Yet he had refused to share that information with anyone else, even Richard, insisting that the contents of the message were Harry's business alone. Nor did he say where they were going. But he seemed to think it urgent that they arrive as fast as possible. Meanwhile, whenever they were forced to stop for a meal or a change of horses, Richard was kind and solicitous, but he seemed deeply preoccupied. Prudence knew that he was fiercely missing Helena and deeply worried about his brother. Was he also regretting taking Lord Belham into their confidence?

Lady Acton remained cool and unruffled, always perfectly groomed and collected. In contrast, Prudence was painfully aware of the shabby state of her clothes and the vast social gulf which lay between a governess and a countess. Yet Harry's mother did not dwell on their difference in either status or appearance. Instead she made amusing, intelligent, and deceptively random conversation.

It was the afternoon of the second day when that changed.

"You must have come to know my son quite well, Miss Drake," Lady Acton said casually as they climbed back into the carriage after lunch at an inn. She settled her skirts on the coach seat and smiled at Prudence. "No doubt you found him capricious at times. As the second son, Harry has always had a great deal to contend with. He will have no title while Richard will become an earl, and Harry inherits nothing, of course, except for what I can leave him of my own money or what his father might choose to give him from the secondary properties. The entire estate of King's Acton is entailed with the earldom, and Lord Acton's mother even left Acton Mead to Richard, as well. Harry was Richard's heir until he married, of course. But when Helena has a son, Harry's future narrows with absolute certainty.''

Prudence looked up at the countess and swallowed her sudden consternation. Did Lady Acton have a deeper purpose in telling her that Harry was entirely dependent on his father's good will? This could hardly be idle conversation. In fact, none of Lady Acton's conversation had seemed idle to Prudence. Since they had left Acton Mead, she had felt that she was being very carefully, though very gently, examined. ''Is Harry envious of Richard?''

The black eyes met hers. ''Oh, no, I don't think so. Richard always loved him too well, you see. There is a deeper bond between my sons than there is between either of them and their father. But Lord Acton has wished that Harry was the heir since the day he arrived and never troubled to hide his partiality. It wasn't easy for the boys.''

Prudence thought briefly of her own brothers and sisters. They had never for one moment thought that their parents had a favorite, but of course there hadn't been any earldom to inherit. ''Lord Acton preferred Harry to Richard? Why?''

Lady Acton adjusted her gloves. ''Because when he was born, Acton wasn't sure that Richard was his own son.''

Prudence was shocked into silence. She studied the elegant line of the countess's traveling dress and the enchanting curve of her neck and jaw. She was so beautiful! Twenty-five years ago she must have been stunning. *Lady Felicity Roseleigh before her marriage—one of the famous Roseleigh roses immortalized by Gainsborough, the beautiful daughters of the late Duke of Bydover*. Was Lady Acton admitting to infidelity to her husband?

''Lord Acton is very English—fair hair, blue eyes—he

thought that his child should look exactly like him. Instead Richard has my eyes. They were black even when he was a baby. In the earl's mind it raised questions. Of course, he also knew that I loved someone else.'' The countess glanced up and laughed openly at Prudence's dismay. ''You come from a staid Scottish home, don't you? Don't let me shock you. Such things are common enough among us, I'm afraid. One of my own sisters has given each of her offspring a different father. Acton was insecure and jealous because he was ten years my senior and ours was an arranged marriage, but I am not a fool. My children are all my husband's. It became obvious enough as Richard grew older, but Harry remained the favorite. It has been a dreadful burden to him, I'm afraid.''

''That his father favored him?''

''Of course. To a child of Harry's temperament it was hateful to see the earl unfairly punish the brother he loved or only blame Richard when they both ran into mischief. Lord Acton also demanded a level of perfection in Harry which would have broken a less gifted child. It is an agony to him if he thinks he has let those standards down. Have you ever seen him shoot?''

''Yes! He was testing new pistol designs for Mr. MacEwen at the Manse.''

The countess glanced from the window. ''It is almost frightening, isn't it? Such a passion for accuracy and faultlessness! Harry needs to learn that he can fail, that he's also only human. I am so glad that he never went to war as Richard did. The Peninsular Campaign almost destroyed Richard. Helena saved him.''

''Lady Acton, why are you telling me this?''

Harry's mother laughed. ''Because I have seen enough of the world and far too much of love, my dear. Harry is more precious to me than I can tell you, and I would sacrifice anyone or anything for him. But my sons are hard on women. When Richard married Helena, I thought he would break her heart— I tried to warn her. And he very nearly did, but because she loved him Helena did not give up. I know you love Harry. I am asking you not to fail him—not to give up, whatever he might do.''

Prudence felt the blush start somewhere at the base of her neck and burn slowly up her cheeks. She wanted to disappear. ''How can you know?'' she said at last. ''And how can you possibly approve?''

Lady Acton's voice was very soft, but quite serious. ''As soon as you mentioned Harry's name when I found you there in Richard's curricle, I knew it with certainty. And you spent how many weeks alone with him? Harry is far too attractive to women. I have seen females with far more sophistication than you lose their hearts to him, my dear. But don't think I approve of marriage between you. How could I? The earl would never allow it—and apart from anything else he controls Harry's allowance and his future security. But my son's happiness is paramount with me, Miss Drake. If Harry wants you and you love him, for heaven's sake at least become his mistress.''

Prudence felt as if she were being attacked by a battery of guns. Yet Lady Acton meant no cruelty, she was only speaking the truth. Nevertheless, Prudence burned with a hot rush of rage. ''How do you know that I have not already done so?''

Lady Acton raised a delicate brow. ''Do you really believe that I cannot recognize a virgin?''

''Then you think I should sacrifice my honor in a vain attempt to offer love to Harry?''

Lady Acton turned to her with something very close to ferocity. ''Is bedding a man such a huge thing? It's been done since the dawn of time, my dear, and by better women than you. You love him, and Harry has too much honor to leave you in want. Why not? He would provide for you even after he married.''

''He would despise me, and more importantly, he would despise himself!''

''Dear God! I have talked with Richard. Something has happened which is eating Harry alive. I don't know what it is, but

I am afraid of what he might do. Lord Acton wants him to marry one of the Salisbury girls and in some wild gesture of conciliation to his father, he might do it. They are grasping, cold-hearted creatures. Either of them could damage him beyond repair—especially if he had nowhere else to go to for warmth.''

"You think I could give him that warmth?" Prudence was almost choking. "That taking someone like me for a mistress would prevent that?"

"It might. Yet I will not see my children forced into loveless marriages as I was, just because they have the misfortune to be earl's sons."

But he wanted to marry me! thought Prudence. *Should I have accepted? Was it some kind of selfish, foolish pride that I did not? He cannot help it that he loves Helena. What man would not? But even without that, Harry's father would destroy him if he married without his consent!* She watched Lady Acton wring a hand across her eyes, and realized with sudden insight quite how much this conversation must be costing Harry's mother. "You did not love Lord Acton at all?"

The countess glanced up at Prudence. She arched a graceful brow and smiled with something close to derision. It made her look very like her son. "No, of course not. I was in love with someone else, but my father wouldn't hear of a match between us. Acton knew how I felt, of course, which is why he was jealous. But Richard was his child."

So this elegant, cool countess had known some very deep suffering of her own. What sympathy could Prudence possibly offer that wouldn't sound clumsy? "Harry told me your father was the Duke of Bydover. That's a very powerful place in the peerage, isn't it? Wasn't it natural that he would want the most consequence for you?"

"The most consequence! No, he wanted the most respectability. The man I loved had too wild a reputation for my father's taste. In spite of his splendid prospects, he was known as a rake and a gambler—and he was very nearly involved in a huge public scandal.'' Her lip curled. ''But he was destined to be a higher lord than the Earl of Acton; he was the eldest son of a marquess.''

Prudence knew that she was scarlet. ''A marquess?''

''Indeed, my dear. I was sixteen and he was only twenty, with all the brittle pride of youth. Yet he begged my father for my hand, swore to reform, to submit to any condition—however humiliating—if we could marry. He even offered to wait until I was older, so that he could prove himself. My father forbade him the house. I was married to Acton within the month, yet when Richard arrived the earl thought that he might be a lover's child. The man's eyes were as black as mine, you see. As black as Richard's. Haven't you guessed?''

The carriage ran on through the English countryside for a few moments in perfect silence, except for the creaking of leather and wood and the rhythmic beat of the horses' hooves.

Prudence took a deep breath, for her emotions threatened to suffocate her. ''It was Lord Belham? Lady Acton, I'm so sorry. I don't know what to say.''

Harry's mother was gazing calmly from the window, but her voice burned with passion. ''Yet you are still worried that Lord Belham means harm to my son! Now you will see that such a thing is preposterous, because the marquess is still in love with me. I also know it is impossible that he intends harm to the child, for I know what Belham is and what is in his soul. So put your mind at rest, Miss Drake. Lord Belham is not your villain. Secondly, I want you to know why I don't believe in marriages arranged for reasons of property and status. Once I was wed, Lord Belham also married someone else. She died in childbirth, heartbroken, a year later. My father's demands ruined all of our lives. I shall not let my husband's expectations ruin my children's.'' She turned to Prudence. The beautiful black eyes were blurred with tears. ''If you love Harry, Miss Drake, I expect you to help me.''

*   *   *

The miles passed in a blur. They reached Glasgow late in the evening. For the first time, Lord Belham announced that they would stop for the night. Prudence was shown into her own spacious chamber where, from sheer exhaustion, she fell asleep instantly in the huge feather bed. In the morning the English carriages were left at the inn. They were to travel on into the Highlands in a narrow-axle carriage which Lord Belham hired for the purpose.

"I learned the last time," he said dryly, "that I'd have been better to have left my own coach and four behind. The roads out of Glasgow were built to accommodate soldiers marching on foot. They are the very devil on a decent coach."

"The last time?" asked Prudence.

He looked at her and laughed. "Indeed, Miss Drake. Where did you think we were going? I have very recently discovered just how bad is the road to Dunraven. I'm damned if I want to walk there again."

A gilt-green tinge delicately decorated the landscape. Most of the snow had melted, except in pockets on the high peaks. The stone walls of Dunraven Castle seemed to smile in the spring sunshine like an old gray cat. As the little cavalcade drew up before the massive oak doors, Prudence stared at them. Why did she want Bobby to come into this inheritance? She had only lived here for two months and never left these hulking walls and barren courtyards. It was a grim enough place for a small child!

Geordie leaned from the top of the wall and glared down at them, his white hair shining like snow.

"So it's yon black laird again? Lady Dunraven does nae want to see ye! Ye can gang awa' again, back whence ye came!"

Lord Belham grinned. "Miss Drake is with me, sir. You

remember her, pray? She has a report for the dowager countess on the state of little Lord Dunraven's health. Surely Lady Dunraven will open the gates to her own grandson's governess?''

Prudence climbed out of the carriage and waved up at the wizened face. "It is me, Geordie! Pray open the gates!''

The retainer peered at her, his eyes shaded against the sun. Then he shrugged, his face disappeared, and a few moments later the great gates creaked open. The carriage lumbered through into the echoing stone courtyard, and the travelers heard the great gates of Dunraven Castle thud shut behind them.

They passed in single file under an archway and through narrow passageways into the solid, grim heart of the keep. The dowager Countess of Dunraven stood in front of her huge fireplace. She was dressed entirely in black. In the dim light filtering through the ancient arrow-slit windows her white hair glimmered with an oddly pure intensity, but her face was rigid. She looked at each of them with clear disdain.

"Do you offer us no welcome, Countess?" asked Lord Belham. "May I present Lady Acton and Lord Lenwood? Miss Drake you know, of course.''

"I did not expect to see you at my hearth again, sir!'' Lady Dunraven glowered at the marquess. "Not again in this lifetime. You are not welcome here! I would to God I had directed my servants to set the dogs on you!''

"Oh, for heaven's sake,'' said Lady Acton. She crossed the room and deliberately took a seat. Prudence watched her remove her bonnet, so that a thin shaft of sunlight highlighted her rich black hair. Harry's mother was still elegant, still cool, still beautiful. With the sun behind her, she looked no more than five-and-twenty. "Are we to have melodrama? I did not expect you to have changed in all these years, Lady Dunraven, but I hoped you had at least found peace with yourself. If you cannot feel any genuine pleasure at our arrival, surely you can at least offer a modicum of courtesy to visitors?''

Lady Dunraven stalked up to Harry's mother and glared down at her. "You dare to talk to me of civility or decorum, Lady Acton? You seem happy enough to travel with your old lover without shame! Or are you lovers yet?"

The marquess calmly walked up to them and stood beside Lady Acton. His features were a perfect mask, but his voice cut with deadly incisiveness. "Don't bother to slander Lady Acton with your poisonous invective, Countess. She and I have not been private together for over twenty years—since before you came back here to live out your widowhood in Scotland. Have you spent all that time alone at Dunraven and tormented yourself with lurid fancies? Is that why you drove away your own son as soon as he was old enough to leave you? How ironic that he should come straight to me to confess his misery. No wonder when he was dying of consumption he appointed me his son's legal guardian. Yet you sent his orphaned child away into the world with no more protection than this naive young woman. Who the devil are you to talk about shame?"

"So what is this?" Lady Dunraven swept out an arm and pointed at Prudence. "The child's governess arrives without the child!"

"Do you truly think that Bobby should be brought back here and placed under *your* tender care, Lady Dunraven?"

The room throbbed with tension.

Lady Dunraven spun around and dropped into the huge ornate chair beside the fireplace. Hatred was plain on her face as she stared up at the marquess. "So have you murdered the child already, Lord Belham? Do you bring me proof of the deed and demand your inheritance as his heir?"

With an unconscious courtesy Richard had moved closer to Prudence. She felt his steady strength next to her with heartfelt gratitude. What on earth was going on? Richard's quick, intelligent glance had flickered once from his mother to Lord Belham. The vertical line was etched deeply between his brows. "Lord Dunraven is perfectly safe, madam," he said calmly. "He is in England at my home, Acton Mead, and receiving the best of care. My wife is with him. We thought another journey so soon too much for such a young child.''

The dowager laughed with open scorn. ''And who are you, sir? Some upstart rogue, no doubt, who conspires the ruin of Dunraven and the destruction of my house!''

''Oh, no, your ladyship,'' said a subtle voice from the doorway. ''The gentleman you are maligning with such thoroughness is my brother. Hello, Richard. Your servant, Miss Drake, Lord Belham.''

Harry stepped into the room and leaned back against the wall. His face was very white and his dark hair fell in disheveled disarray over his forehead. He carelessly ran both hands back through it, and obviously suppressed a wince. With clear reluctance he looked up and the harebell eyes glanced past Prudence to gaze straight at Lady Acton. They were filled with pain and a deadly, blank recoil. ''And Mother? How very amiable to see you, also. So what the devil brings you all running after me like a gaggle of fluffy little goslings clacking after the hen wife? Any bread crumbs you get from me will stick in the craw like stones, I assure you.''

Chapter 13

Richard had taken Prudence by the arm and helped her to a chair. Harry had dropped onto a long settle and spread his arms carelessly along the back. No one else had moved. Prudence stared woodenly at her knees, forcing herself not to faint or weep or otherwise disgrace herself. Meaningless snatches of prayer raced through her mind. *Oh, dear God! What had happened now?* Then her head snapped up as Richard crossed the room to stand threateningly over Harry.

"You will be pleased to apologize, sir, to your mother."

"Oh, Lord," said Harry. "Are we to have histrionics? And if I will not, noble brother, you will make me?"

"I don't believe that should be necessary, sir. You will kindly remember your manners and speak to our mother with a civil tongue, that is all."

"And to my father?" asked Harry. With deliberate insolence he stared straight at Lord Belham. "Do I owe civility to the unprincipled man who took our mother to his bed and sired her a bastard for a second son?"

Richard slapped him hard across the face.

Lady Acton leapt to her feet. "Richard!"

Harry's head cracked back to strike the hard edge of the settle. He broke into feral, uncontrolled laughter. "By God, if anyone else wants to hit me over the head, I wish they would do it now and get it over with. Stay out of this, Richard. It's none of your damned business!"

"If you do not take back your outrageous insult to our mother, Harry, I shall call you out and damn the consequences!"

"Richard!" Lady Acton had run up to her eldest son and caught him by the sleeve. "Do not be so absurd! Harry is a crack shot. He would kill you!"

"And if your daughter-in-law's coming baby is female or if she loses the child from the shock of hearing of her husband's untimely death, Harry would be the next earl!" The dowager countess laughed with open triumph. "Unless I tell the world what I have already told him. Harry is a bastard, isn't he, Lady Acton? And his father is the man you couldn't wait to take to your bed when you were scarce sixteen years old. When you couldn't have him in marriage, you had him four years later in adulterous lust. Harry's father is not your husband, the Earl of Acton, he's my charming nephew, my husband's sister's son: none other than Lord Belham! Now, isn't that a delicious situation!"

There was a dreadful, echoing silence. Prudence longed to go to Harry. She wanted to hold him, to kiss him, to do anything to ease the agony that she saw in his features. Instead she sat on her wooden chair as if doomed to live out her days in its callous embrace.

"I don't believe it," said Richard. His features seemed somehow blurred, attenuated by shock.

"Neither did I, at first, but unfortunately there is proof. Lady Dunraven gave me this." Harry reached into his jacket pocket and brought out a sheet of paper. It was yellowed and faded. He handed it to Richard. "Read it, Richard, by all means. Everyone here knows what it contains, except you and Miss Drake."

Richard glanced over it. "This is part of a letter?" He turned to Lord Belham. "Sir, the signature is yours."

Lord Belham still stood as if turned to stone. His voice seemed to come from a great distance, but he smiled. "Read my damnation aloud, Lenwood, for God's sake. Lady Dunraven chooses to orchestrate a farce and plans to win whether we admit the truth or not. So why hide anything from this company?"

Richard's black eyes met his mother's. Lady Acton nodded her head and dropped back to her seat. She seemed unmoved, but there was a small frown of anxiety marring her forehead. He glanced back at his brother. "Very well, Harry," he said, his face like granite, and began to read.

" 'It is with very great regret, sir, that I am obliged to inform you that your suspicions and accusations are correct. The countess's son, Henry, is indeed my child, the fruit of an adulterous liaison between us. Nevertheless, the earl is not to know. The boy will be raised as his legitimate offspring. In spite of your revulsion, sir, for my behavior in this instance, I do most earnestly beg that you will divulge this truth to no one, for the sake of the child. His mother's shame is hers to bear, while my own is yours to punish as you see fit . . .' "

Harry interrupted. "Enough, Richard, surely. What a dreadful irony to think that your father, Lord Acton, preferred me to you, his own son! All those damned lessons, all that proud bombast about my achievements, all that intense pressure to fulfill his expectations, wasted on another man's get." He stared insolently up at Lord Belham. "Do you deny that this letter was written by you, my lord? The first page is missing, but your name would appear to be at the end. Please don't tell me that it's a forgery."

"The signature is mine," said the marquess. He was very calm. "Written to my own father. Though it does not mean what you think, I would have given my right hand not to have had this come out, even now. Such things are best left buried forever, for what the hell can be achieved now except hurt to innocent parties?'' He turned to Lady Acton. ''Felicity, can you ever forgive me, my dear?''

The countess stared up at him, her eyes blurred with tears. Then she rose abruptly from her seat and walked over to the small arrow-slit window.

''These windows are designed for warfare, not for light,'' she said into the appalled silence. Then she spun about and fixed her second son with her black gaze. ''But you were wrong about everyone here knowing about this letter and its contents, Harry. I did not.''

There was a knocking at the door into the room. Prudence turned to look at the innocent oak planks as if the sound were the knell of doom.

The door opened and a face peered in. ''Well, Lady Dunraven,'' said the newcomer. ''It would seem that Mr. Harry Acton's family have run him to earth. I trust I don't intrude, but it seemed they might want to meet the villain that nabbed him.''

They all turned to look at him.

It was the man with the eye-patch.

For a moment there was perfect silence.

A stranger. A man who knew nothing of old scandals or family secrets. A man obviously from another world—as far removed from the *beau monde* as the orient.

Richard was the first to recover. The color had drained from his face, but he left Harry and strode over to the man with fists clenched. ''Damn you for a black-hearted brute, sir! Am I to take it that you were responsible for kidnapping my brother after having him beaten?''

''This man intended me no harm, Richard,'' interrupted Harry with deadly authority. ''There was just a little trouble controlling the enthusiasm of the hired accomplices. Thanks to him, it was only one blow—and I asked for it. I was indulging in my unfortunate tendency of being abominably irritating.

Besides, our villain knows you. I was sickened with infatuated and glowing accounts of your martial exploits all the way from the Chilterns to Argyle.''

Richard hesitated as he gazed into the man's face.

"Captain Acton, ain't it?" The man with the eye-patch grinned at him and saluted. "Lord Lenwood as Harry tells me you're rightly called. I knew you in the Peninsula, my lord, though you wouldn't know me now." He touched the eye-patch. "Lost this at Badajoz. That was a rum do, wasn't it, my lord? I knew Mr. Acton was your brother all along. Assure you I'd never have let him get hurt if I could have stopped it.''

"By God, Sergeant Keen!" Richard visibly relaxed, and once again the calm control slipped over his features. "I remember you for a brave man. Badajoz took finer lives than either of ours. I'm sorry about your wound, Sergeant. You were sent home afterwards, of course. But you were a damned good soldier—why the hell have you now taken to a life of crime?"

Sergeant Keen was instantly offended. "Wasn't any crime, my lord, to track down Mr. Acton and bring him to Dunraven. He'd contracted in France to fetch a paper to Lady Dunraven and was just being helped to keep his word as a gentleman. You wouldn't want your brother forsworn, now, would you?"

"Sergeant Keen did not know that I had lost my memory, Richard," said Harry with a grin. "He thought I was just being awkward."

"You were bringing the paper to Lady Dunraven, Harry?" asked Lady Acton.

Prudence watched with astonishment as the countess gracefully moved back across the room as if this were merely a social gathering. *Dear Lord! Are they all so expert at concealing their emotions—at revealing no weakness before the lower orders? But what about me? I am no more a member of the peerage than Sergeant Keen!*

The countess sat down and began to laugh. "Oh, dear heavens preserve us. Very well, let us have this little mystery out, at least. What was in the paper?"

"A formula for a fulminate mixture and a plan for a new firing mechanism," said Harry. As controlled now as Richard, he spoke of it with calm, casual nonchalance. "I obtained it in France from a master gunsmith." He glanced at his brother. "That is where I went after Madame Relet's little fire. The man turned up as if by magic when I was looking for any excuse not to come straight home. I worked with him on some experiments with the new percussion systems. If only we could contain the charge in a reliable cap which would fire when hit by a hammer, we could do away with flint and priming pan and all the attendant drawbacks of our flintlock pistols. Imagine! A weapon which never misfired or flashed in the pan, and would be reliable in any weather or any conditions. The gunsmith in France thought he had the perfect mixture at last and he had been in correspondence with Lady Dunraven about it. It would have been noble espionage, perhaps, when we were at war with France, but we were entirely at peace in February when I agreed to bring the formula to Scotland. Napoleon was imprisoned and the Bourbons solidly on the throne. There was nothing terribly heroic about it, I'm afraid." Harry glanced at his mother. "Nor did I know anything of a family connection to Lady Dunraven, except that Dunraven Castle seemed a long way from Acton Mead."

Lady Acton stared directly at the dowager countess. "No doubt you chose my son as a messenger quite deliberately. What a perfect chance to strike back at me! How could he have known of any link between us? This French gunsmith must have made such a convenient agent for you, knowing Harry's fame as a dead shot and his natural interest in firearms. But you are surely not going to tell me that you have spent all these years experimenting with guns, Lady Dunraven?"

The dowager countess turned to her in open triumph. "That is exactly what I have been doing. The patent for the first truly reliable percussion cap will be worth a fortune! And of course when I had word he was in France and looking for some exploit on which to waste his talents I took the chance to meet your son. It seemed to have a perfect symmetry. Unfortunately Harry is as untrustworthy as the rest of your clan. He was shipwrecked, he says. I sent Sergeant Keen after him when he failed to arrive here. But the formula and plan have been lost.''

''I came from France in a small private boat,'' said Harry. The dead-calm control was still there. Prudence found it almost more frightening than his earlier display of passion. ''We were shipwrecked in a storm—the boat went down with all hands, I imagine, but I was cast up on the beach where Miss Drake found me. When I remembered that I was supposed to be carrying it, the paper was already gone. So Sergeant Keen tracked me up and down England to no avail. This entire adventure has been an exercise in folly and a wild goose chase.''

''But the paper was not lost, Harry.'' Lady Acton folded her fan. She was looking at Harry with an odd longing. ''Miss Drake found it and sent it to London. Now Lord Belham has it.''

Harry looked up with intense surprise. ''Prudence! Lord Belham? How on earth?''

Prudence could not watch Harry's face. This was surely the last nail to hammer down any vestige of feeling he might have had for her. She had betrayed him to his enemy—had not trusted him enough to show him what she had found in his coat. And that supposed enemy, Lord Belham, was his own father. She closed her eyes for a moment. That revelation about his family made her totally irrelevant, didn't it? It was an enormity that could never be forgiven. Lady Acton had lied to her during their journey, but how much worse if for four-and-twenty years she had lied to Harry? Richard very probably was Lord Acton's son, but not all of her children were her husband's. The countess had forsaken her wedding vows for her first love and born him a son. It was too overwhelming, too much to take in, and far too much to think about clearly. Prudence only knew that she ached for Harry, and for herself, and for every stupid misunderstanding and mistake they had ever shared.

Lady Acton turned to the marquess. ''For heaven's sake, put

us out of our misery, sir. Is the flintlock firearm about to be made obsolete? Has Harry single-handedly put the future into our hands?''

Lord Belham glanced up at her, remote, cool. Yet the air thrummed between them. "It will be obsolete in ten years, Lady Acton. There is no question about it. And some of us in government are watching and encouraging every experiment designed toward that aim. But it will not be made so by Harry's secret French missive." His dark gaze swept across the room to Harry. "I had wished to impart such an embarrassing fact to you in private, sir, but it seems we are all destined to wash our dirty linen in the market square today. The paper which Miss Drake sent to London indeed contained plans for a new pistol design and formula, but not one which will work to the purpose. It has already been tried and has failed completely. I'm sorry, sir. Here, you may have it, if you wish."

He reached into his coat and pulled out a wrinkled, soiled scrap of paper. Prudence recognized it immediately.

"But that's mine!" cried Lady Dunraven. "Harry Acton was supposed to bring it to me!" She imperiously reached out a hand.

Lord Belham placed the paper in her palm. "By all means, madam. I admit when I first realized what it was I thought it might be valuable, but it is entirely spurious. Make of it what you may."

"You mean," said Sergeant Keen scratching his head, "that all my hard work was for nothing?"

"So it would seem, sir." Harry began to laugh. "And your highwayman friend hit me over the head for even less. Confess, now, everyone, that this has been a singular piece of folly and I'm damned if I can stay here to hear any more. You will excuse me, Mother, your ladyship, my lord."

"One moment, Harry." It was Lady Acton.

He turned his head to her with a painful reluctance.

"You said you were looking for any excuse not to come home. Why, pray? Why stay in France at all?"

Harry stood up and smiled at her, a deadly, chilling, soulless smile. "Because I thought I was in love with Helena. And I didn't want to do to my own brother what my father did to Lord Acton. Of course, I didn't know at that time about your splendid example, or that such blood would taint my veins. Without question Helena has eyes for no one but Richard, so I doubt if there was much danger. Nevertheless, those were my reasons at the time. I'm sure you will think them the reasons of a fool."

He bowed with elaborate grace and left the room. He had not once glanced at Prudence.

Lady Dunraven stared at the message which Harry had brought from France. "Someone has made a mistake!"

"No mistake, madam." Lord Belham turned to Sergeant Keen. "By all means take the plan and try it, sir."

The man with the eye-patch saluted. As she held it out, he took the paper from Lady Dunraven's stiff fingers, and left them.

Prudence wanted to leave also, to escape—anything rather than sit here in this grim stone keep and watch a family destroyed by the discovery of an ancient, tragic scandal. She glanced up at Lady Acton, expecting to see that lovely face ravished by the revelation which had just been made. Instead the countess seemed merely very angry. Two spots of bright color burned in her cheeks, making her black eyes extremely bright. Her voice when she spoke was pitched very clear and low, with a bite like a steel blade.

"How dare you, Lady Dunraven! I didn't think that even you would stoop so low. I could not speak freely before Sergeant Keen. You have succeeded, of course, in causing me pain as you wished. I can forgive that, for many years ago it was I who unwittingly brought pain to you. What I cannot forgive, however, is that you have chosen to strike back at me through my son. For God's sake! For God's sake, you are a withered, embittered old woman. Can you never excuse me for being seventeen years younger than you? Can you never pardon me for loving Lord Belham when I was sixteen? Can you never forgive that he loved me back? He was younger than either of my sons here, and you see how young they are! And I was just a girl who had met her first love—there should have been nothing to stop a match between us. But thanks to you, we each married someone else and broke our hearts over it. Would you so cruelly begrudge us a few months of stolen pleasure, four years later, if we were so weak?''

''Dear God, Mother.'' Richard went to her and dropped on one knee at her feet. ''Don't tell me this is true about Harry?''

Lady Acton laughed and touched his cheek in a gesture of pure love. ''No, of course it's not! You and Harry are full brothers, sir. Much as I may have wished it, I did not bear Lord Belham a son. No, the truth is far worse than that, for though it does not touch upon my honor, it strikes very deeply into my heart. The countess that the marquess wrote to his father about was his aunt, Lady Dunraven. She was thirty-three when she seduced him, a beautiful, worldly thirty-three. And he was only nineteen! They were lovers for almost a year. When he wanted to end it and marry me, she threatened to tell the world and damn the consequences: a criminal conversation suit against her own nephew, son of another peer, and close enough—though not in blood—to be incest! She did tell his father and mine—told them that he had ravished her. And that was the message that my father brought to me, and enough to prevent our marriage. Yet I still loved him.'' Lady Acton leaned forward and kissed Richard on the forehead. ''What I did not know is why she did it—lust for a hale young man? Lady Dunraven never felt any emotion so honest! Nor did I know why this withered old crone went to so much trouble to trap me into coming here now so that she could let me know in front of my sons. But I do now.''

Lady Acton had begun to cry, entirely without shudders. Her black eyes had simply filled with water and tears spilled down her exquisite cheeks. Lord Belham made an odd, broken gesture, but he did not go to her.

"It was in order to get an heir for Dunraven, wasn't it?" asked Lady Acton. She looked away from Richard and stared straight at the dowager countess. "You took a boy into your bed so you would get the son that your husband hadn't given you in twelve years of marriage. Even if he suspected, Lord Dunraven would have kept his silence as long as nothing was made public. His own sister's boy: was that close enough in blood to count as his own? You gained out of it everything that you wanted, used Lord Belham like a harlot, yet you couldn't bear it when he wanted me, Lady Felicity Roseleigh, youngest of the Roseleigh roses. Your beautiful paramour fell in love with a girl closer to his own age and wanted to marry her, and you have never forgiven either of them to this day. You are a sad, pathetic creature, Lady Dunraven. And you always were."

Prudence longed to be anywhere else, but she sat as if pinned to her chair. She groped to make sense of it—all this long-ago scandal, all these passions felt by people now growing old. Love, greed, hatred, did nothing dim with time?

"Then the child of that affair was also named Henry?" asked Richard quietly. He had risen to stand at his mother's shoulder. His face was still very white and set.

"Yes, of course," said Lady Dunraven, her triumph undimmed. "It was my husband's name, the least I could do after making him a cuckold with his own sister's boy. Lord Belham and I had a son together to inherit Dunraven. That is him on the wall over there: Bobby's father, the second Henry and fourth Earl of Dunraven, who died in his father's care this last winter in London. You did not know that, did you, Lady Acton? You did not know that I had a child with the man you loved! He may have told you that I had seduced him. Hah! He did not tell you I bore the seed of his loins."

Richard turned to Lord Belham. His tone was sharp with a mixture of emotions that Prudence couldn't read. "Forgive me, sir. But we are all involved now whether we wish it or not. Am I to understand that you are therefore in truth Bobby's grandfather?''

''Yes,'' replied the marquess. His bones shone stark beneath his skin. ''Bobby is my ward, my second cousin, and my grandson. Now can you all believe that I would never have harmed a hair on his head?''

Prudence knew she shouldn't intervene. That this was deeper and more personal than she had any right to be hearing. But the agony of it was too much!

She rose from her chair and faced Lady Dunraven. ''Why did you send me away with Bobby?'' she cried. ''Why did you tell me his life was in danger? Are you mad?''

''Sit down, Miss Drake! You forget yourself! You are in *my* employ, young woman. Pray, don't forget it.''

Lord Belham came up to her and took her hand. ''Miss Drake. I'm sorry that you should have been subjected to all this. The dowager countess sent Bobby away so that I shouldn't be able to take care of him. Perhaps she's right. The notorious Black Belham is hardly a suitable companion for a five-year-old boy, even if he is the child's grandfather. But I am the new Lord Dunraven's legal guardian and Bobby's future is under my control, not hers. She used you, as she has used people for sixty-two years. It was just a last spiteful gesture from a spurned woman, that's all.''

Lady Acton gazed at him. Her eyes were like dark pools. ''It makes no difference, Alex,'' she said in her beautiful, carefully modulated voice. ''It makes no difference that she bore you a bastard. None at all. We have each of us made a new life since then. Good God, do you think I care anymore that your aunt had more of you than I could ever have? We were children. What the devil did we know of love? No, there is only one thing that matters to me now—''

''Felicity, please!''

She silenced him with a lifted hand. ''And that's Harry! Lady Dunraven has done her damnedest to damage my son.

Life has left us behind, but Harry is the future. I have no tender feelings left for any man, Lord Belham, but I do care very much that Harry is not harmed any more by this old witch! If you had told me at the time that Bobby's father was your son, I might have been more prepared. Instead I have just seen Harry reduced to despair by a letter which you wrote, and was helpless to prevent it. So do not think that I can so easily forgive you, sir.''

"Mother, don't!" It was Richard. "Harry will only have to give all this two hours reflection to know that the marquess isn't his father. No, there's far more than this foolish imbroglio wrong with Harry. I don't think that any of us can mend that!''

"Then what is to be done, Richard?''

Richard looked across the room at Prudence, still sitting stiffly in her chair. "Let Miss Drake go to him.''

"Miss Drake?'' Lady Dunraven stood up and motioned to Prudence. Her white hair shone in the dim light. "Yes, what role has Miss Drake played for the last several weeks? Traveled alone, unchaperoned, with Harry Acton! You have let me down, young woman. You are dismissed from my service and from Dunraven Castle this instant. There will be no references. As far as I am concerned your character stinks like mud.''

Richard ignored her. "You know this place, Miss Drake. You lived here with Bobby, didn't you? Can you guess where Harry might have gone?''

Prudence closed her eyes. She did know. She knew it in her bones and in the tips of her fingers. It was where she would have gone if she was in pain and her world had shattered about her.

"He will be on the battlements,'' she said.

Chapter 14

The stair leading up to the top of Dunraven Keep made a tight spiral in the thickness of the masonry. The curve was such that a right-handed man with a sword had the advantage defending the worn stone steps against attackers coming from below. Prudence grasped her skirts in one hand, running the fingers of the other over the rough stones of the outer wall. There was no handrail, not even a rope. It was a treacherous, dangerous climb for a woman in old, cracked boots and long skirts. Prudence was entirely unaware of that. She only knew that Hal was up there and needed help.

"I have made a bloody fool of myself again, haven't I?" said Harry as Prudence stepped out onto the topmost ramparts of Dunraven Keep.

He was leaning against the merlons. A small, cold breeze running out of the mountains in wild, fey gusts lifted the dark hair from his forehead. He did not turn his head to look at her. He was gazing out across the long waters of the black loch.

Rank upon rank of towering, snow-capped peaks stretched away into the distance, green and gilt-edged grays dissolving to a hazy blue where the mountains met the sky in perfect communion. Harry seemed as remote and as lonely as the hills, his voice cold, his skin pinched white by the breeze and by a chilling, bone-deep fatigue.

Prudence stopped where she was. She felt awkward, dumb. How could she reach him? Did he even want to be reached?

"You know, this is a remarkable landscape, Miss Drake. I am awestruck, humbled, belittled by rocks and water. I should like to dissolve into it, become a runnel of dampness on a cliff face. What is that mountain there? The one that looks like an old woman crouched over her fire?"

"Beinn Mhor—the Big Mountain."

Harry tried to wrap his English tongue around the soft sounds. *"Ben vore."*

He was giving her a way out. A way not to face everything that had happened. A way to be polite strangers and say goodbye politely. She began to name the peaks and valleys. The rolling, lovely Gaelic names: the Mountain of the Aspens, the Moor of Black Crows, the Pass of the Moss. And beyond them lay the sea, the wild beckoning ocean, home of the silkie.

Prudence closed her eyes and felt the cold breeze kiss her cheeks with ice.

"They fall in love with him because he's comely," said Bobby.

"But can his lady never keep him by her side?"

"Only if she can find his fur coat and burn it. Then he's a man forever and she can marry him. But if she doesn't do it right, he dies."

"You owe a great many people an apology," Prudence said harshly. She opened her eyes and made herself look at him. At every loved detail of his face and bones and body, the long, graceful lines of back and leg, and the wild, wind-tossed hair. "Are you too much of a coward to give it?"

Harry spun about and faced her. Strong color washed up

over his face to stain his high cheekbones and emphasize the
deep harebell-blue of his eyes.

"Yes," he said baldly. "What use is an apology when the
act is so damned? Do you think there are words in the language
sufficient to take back what I said to my mother?"

"You want to take them back?"

"Oh, God." Harry covered his face with both hands. "It
wasn't even true, was it? For God's sake! How could I have
believed she would not have told me? Even for a moment?
And I cannot be Belham's son. His eyes are as black as my
mother's."

Prudence was lost. "His eyes! Why does that matter?"

He dropped his hands and revealed his own. They had a
bruised look, cerulean on cobalt, like the mountains fading into
the sky. "Because my eyes are blue, angel. I had a friend at
Oxford who made a study of these things. He found that every
blue-eyed child has at least one blue-eyed parent, like the Saxon
Earl of Acton, my father. Thus I could not be Lord Belham's
byblow—though he is a better man! How the hell could I have
let that old witch deceive me?"

"Lady Dunraven had her own reasons for misleading you
and giving you that letter. She wanted to hurt your mother. She
arranged it, didn't she, so that you didn't have any time to
think about it?"

The flush was fading, to leave him dead white again. "There
is no excuse for what I said."

"You are hurt," said Prudence. "You have been beaten and
injured. You had just read something which left you in shock.
It was only human to react to it."

Harry had turned back to the parapet. He laid a hand, palm
open, fingers splayed, on a merlon on each side of him. His
profile was cut cleanly against the sky.

"Only human? To let emotion override reason and lash out
at those who love you because their love prevents them from
striking back? Then I'm damned if I want to be human, angel."

"Lord Belham wrote that letter to his father almost thirty

years ago. It was about Lady Dunraven. They were lovers before he ever met your mother, but when he did he wanted to marry her. Your grandfather prevented the marriage and broke her heart. Yet your mother didn't know until now that Lord Belham and Lady Dunraven had a child together—Bobby's father. What have you ever done to hurt her which could come close to that? Are you so damned proud that you won't take or offer forgiveness?''

''It's not pride.''

''Isn't it? Then what else is it?''

Harry's fingers were gripping the stone of the battlements as if he would break off pieces and hurl them into space. The bones and tendons stood out starkly on the backs of his hands. Prudence looked at them, those beautiful, elegant hands, still callused from his work on the narrow boat.

''It's shame,'' he said at last, and his voice choked on it.

And then she was devastated, for Harry closed his eyes over cheeks wet with tears. Prudence reacted instantly, without thinking or weighing the consequences. She went to him and pulled his hands away from the stone. He turned blindly to her as she put her arms around his body and held him.

''Let it go, Harry. For heaven's sake, let it go. You are human. You are one of us. Filled with flaws and pettiness and folly. You have made mistakes. You will keep making mistakes. That's what humans do. We strive to be better and only continue to fail. We're just trapped here for a little while in these frail bodies, haunted by our own awareness. It isn't possible to become unaware, like a seal or a running stream. Why are you pretending now that nothing is wrong with you? I saw that man hit you with his pistol. Doesn't your head ache?''

Harry laughed weakly into her hair. His arms were around her back and he was holding her tightly to his chest. ''Like the torments of the damned, angel. I think the grand old Duke of York is marching his ten thousand men up and down in my skull with full drums and bagpipers.''

''Then what is the use of heroics? You must come inside

and lie down. Will you? I will see if there is any willow bark in the kitchen.''

Gently he released her and held her away from him at arm's length. ''Dear Prudence, when did you become such a bully? Very well.''

Harry kept her hand in a tight grasp as he led her back to the head of the stairs. He opened the little wooden door and began to run lightly down ahead of her. Prudence tried to take one step and gulped. The stone center post of the stairs seemed to drop away into nothingness, turning her vision dizzy and her knees to water.

''Hal,'' she gasped.

He stopped and looked up at her. ''What is it?''

''I can't! I shall fall!''

''No, angel. You won't fall. Here, I have your hand. Just bend your knees and take a step.''

Prudence shook her head.

The harebell eyes gravely studied her. ''This is the other thing it takes to be human,'' he said quietly. ''Courage and trust. Do not look down, just look at the place where the wide part of the step meets the wall. I won't let you fall, angel.''

His palm was warm under her own. Warm, reassuring, full of strength. Prudence took a step, then another. With her eyes fixed on Harry's she slowly descended the spiral staircase until they arrived on the top floor of the keep.

''Where is your room?'' said Harry.

''No, I'm all right, really! Let us get you some willow!''

''Prudence, leave me to my own demons. You too are exhausted, worn down, stretched thin as a sail in the wind. It is you who needs to lie down.''

Prudence allowed him to lead her along the hallway and into her room.

As she sank into a chair, he kneeled at the hearth and set a spark to the fire. She wanted to reach out and touch his shoulder.

Instead she gathered more courage and readied herself to strip off another layer.

"It's not done yet, Hal. Neither of us will rest until all of it is faced."

Still crouching, he spun on his heel and stared up at her. "You don't know what I've done, angel. You don't know what I am."

"Then tell me. Let me judge for myself. Who are you to decide what I shall or shall not condemn!"

Harry sat back on the hearth rug. He leaned into the base of a heavy settle and stretched his legs in front of him so that his boots were almost touching her skirts. The bruised, tired lids dropped over the blue eyes as if he couldn't bear to see her reaction to what he would say.

"I was my father's favorite child. I never let him down. Nor did I ever willingly let my brother down. Last winter, when Richard was being hunted by an enemy, I dropped everything to help him where I could."

"And you saved his life. I know."

Harry shrugged. "I am lucky enough to be a dead shot, that's all. Better by far than Richard. He doesn't mind. But he had left a failure behind him in Paris, a brothel filled with English children that he hadn't been able to shut down. I was so damned cocksure that I could do better I went there myself."

"And?"

"I shut it down. I burned it to the ground, in fact."

"Was anyone killed?"

"No."

Prudence hugged her arms around her own body. She was glad that he couldn't see her. It made it easier to talk to him as if she had the right to do it. "Then why this anguish, Hal? What is this about?"

His voice was very soft, but he did not hesitate or stumble over the words. "It's about failing myself, I suppose. In order to get the trust of the madam, I became her lover. She liked using young men. My degradation was her pleasure. Can you understand that?''

It was as if the words were dropping into a deep well, and she couldn't understand them until they reached the bottom. Then the water roared up in a great wave as the words hit. ''I don't know. Yes, I think I can.''

''It touched too deep, angel. I hated her for what she did and for what she was, but I wasn't left detached and distant, as I thought I'd be. I foolishly believed I could handle it, that it would be amusing, even if maybe a little distasteful—like putting on a wet greatcoat when you're already chilled. After all, I've had lovers before. It wasn't like that. In spite of everything I knew about Madame Relet, and everything I wanted to believe about myself, my body responded with pleasure to her touch and I found myself wanting her, even as I was disgusted at my own reaction.'' He covered his face with his hands and wrung the long fingers over the drawn skin of his cheeks. ''What the hell does that say about me, do you suppose?''

The ripples at the bottom of the well spread away in ever-widening circles, carrying her with them into an unknown darkness. ''That you're a man, I should think,'' said Prudence.

His head flew up and the blue eyes looked into hers with open astonishment.

''I have two brothers, one in the navy and one in the army. We are very close; they tell me things.'' Prudence could feel her heart pounding like a blacksmith's hammer. ''That is an ability that men have, isn't it, to separate lust from love, or even from conscious desire. If you had not found something in you which wanted her, you couldn't have satisfied her and rescued the little English girls. Why do you torture yourself about it? You had a natural male reaction to a skillful harlot. But don't your motives count? Isn't it how you acted on it that matters?''

Harry moved faster than she could react, so that he was kneeling at her feet with both of her hands imprisoned in his.

His eyes bored into her face. "Angel, I can't believe this. You are not shocked?"

Prudence looked down at him, at the ridge of his nose, the lush eyelashes, the defined curve of his upper lip. "Yes, I'm very shocked. But I was forewarned. Helena told me something about this business, you see. And with Helena, too, your actions were honorable, though you were afraid of your feelings."

"But I am afraid, angel. Afraid I am no better than those men who came to Madame Relet's as clients. How fine a line separates us!"

But if she doesn't do it right, he dies. "We traveled together and shared a bed," said Prudence desperately. "If you were not different from those men, then I would not still be a virgin. Unless your flirtation was all idle nonsense, after all, like your proposal, and you didn't really want me."

Harry slid his hands up her arms and pulled her forward from the chair. Prudence closed her eyes as she tumbled onto him and they fell back together onto the hearth rug in a tangle of skirts. Flames flared up the chimney in the sudden rush of air, and she heard his next words dropped clear and clean, to wash their import over her head and drown her.

"Oh, I want you, angel. Do you need me to prove it?"

Lord Belham turned to face the woman who had taken his virginity. Lady Dunraven glared back.

"You cannot hurt me anymore," he said. "And in trying, you have only hurt yourself. All of Dunraven, these lochs and mountains, woods and fields, this keep and the house that our son Henry built, are Bobby's. I am his guardian in law and management of his estates falls to me. You were right to accuse me of wanting to turn you from your home, Lady Dunraven. I didn't then, but I do now. I don't want you this close to Bobby when he comes home. You will be pleased to pack your things. You may have use of the house in Edinburgh and I will make you an allowance suitable to your station. Think how much you will enjoy that gossipy, close-knit little world. You can blacken my name to your heart's content, and the Edinburgh biddies will enjoy every shudder. Now, get out of my sight!''

Her face as white as her hair, Lady Dunraven drew herself up with undiminished dignity and left the room.

''Good heavens,'' said Lady Acton. ''Do you suppose it would be possible to ring for some tea?''

''Harry wants to marry her, Mother.''

Lady Acton turned to Richard and raised an elegant brow. ''What? Who?''

''Harry wants to marry Miss Drake. He isn't in love with Helena anymore—in spite of what he said—he's in love with Prudence Drake. How the devil are we going to get Father's approval for the wedding?''

''Richard, please be realistic! Acton will *never* allow it! And you know quite well that I don't have that much influence with him.''

''I married Helena without his permission and he forgave us.''

''Yes, but Helena turned out to have property. She had perfectly respectable connections. There is no comparison.''

Richard looked down at his hands, the vertical line deep between his brows. ''No, of course not. For even though I am the heir, Father didn't really care who I married. It is only Harry who must do no wrong. Well, it's been nearly enough to destroy him all his life. He must be allowed to be free of that.''

''Richard, it's not something I can change!''

''Can't you, Mother? Well, it's something I intend to change if I can.''

Lord Belham had crossed to the window and was gazing out through the slim arrow slit. Now he turned and walked back to face them.

''Should I offer to interfere? For God's sake, far be it from me to stand by while young lovers are separated by convention and their parents. Isn't Harry of age?''

"Yes, of course." It was Lady Acton. She gazed up at her first love without artifice, and her lovely eyes were clouded with concern. "But the earl controls his allowance and the secondary properties which might be left to Harry or given to him on his marriage. I do not speak without due knowledge, Alex. If Harry marries this Scottish girl, his father will turn his picture to the wall. He will be penniless and be struck from the will."

"But not from his family," said Richard. "I can make him a small allowance, and more than that. When Father dies I shall be earl. I suppose I'll have to move to King's Acton. Then Harry and Prudence can have Acton Mead."

"Richard! But you love Acton Mead!"

He shrugged. "I love Harry more."

"And in the meantime? I know you will be generous, but Harry won't let himself live off his brother's charity."

"There is another solution." Lord Belham turned to them and smiled. "We are very busy plotters, aren't we? But how do we know that Harry will ask her, or that Miss Drake will accept him if he does?"

Harry rolled Prudence onto her back and pinned her there with one leg across hers. He leaned on one elbow and looked down at her while he stroked the hair back from her forehead with his hand.

"I want to marry you, Miss Drake."

Prudence shook her head.

"Why not? Don't you want me?"

"How can you ask me now? You are ill, and exhausted, and—"

"Mad with lust? Yes, I'm tired, so are you. So we are seeing each other at our worst. What harm in that? For I have just recognized something that I suppose I was just too deuced foolish to see before. Thanks to you and Madame Relet."

"What is that?" Prudence longed to reach up and touch his

face, the strong contours of jaw and nose, the crease left by the dimple in his cheek.

"The difference between love and lust."

"And?" said Prudence.

"There isn't any. That is, love isn't something which exists in contrast to lust. They can be separate but they can also be together. As they are now. I love you, Prudence, but I want you very badly in my bed. Will you marry me?"

"Harry, I can't!"

"Not because of Helena, surely?"

Prudence gazed up into his face. "Lord Jervin told me."

"Ah, I was afraid he might have done." He grinned at her, and Prudence saw how stripped he was by emotion and fatigue. Nothing could remain between them now but truth. "What I felt for her was love, certainly. It still is. But there was never lust in it, or this soul-stirring desire and knowledge that I have met a *partner*. She dazzled me a little, because I'd never met a woman like her. Now I've met one better, I know that what I feel for Helena is right and perfect, and has nothing to do with how I feel for you. Marry me, angel!"

She knew he spoke with absolute candor. To know that he had felt and acted as he had about his brother's wife only made her love him more. Who would not love Helena? But how many men would have worked to save that brother's life and marriage in the face of it as Harry had done? "Your father will destroy you!"

"He can't. He can take away my money. No doubt he will. I shall earn us a living. Why not? That's what second sons do."

"Not second sons of earls!"

"Of course they do. In the army, often enough."

"You will not join the army!"

"No, I don't think so. But I shall find us somewhere and something. What the devil do position and wealth matter without love? Now, say you will marry me!"

"Harry, you must give this more thought!"

"I have given it every ounce of my attention, Prudence. I know what it will mean and I don't ask lightly. But if there is any material sacrifice for me I make it willingly, and I assure you I can give you a more secure future than you have now as a governess. Don't you love me?"

Prudence closed her eyes to block the tears. "With all my heart, Harry."

She felt his lips touch hers with infinite tenderness and his body seemed to melt next to her, so that she fit against him. He held her face still in his hands while the kisses became deeper, burning into her blood with a pure flame. She knew her lips were becoming swollen. Harry kept kissing her. He kissed her as his hands ran over her body, pulling her against him, exploring the curve of her back and waist—and then her breast, and her soft thigh, and the swell of her buttock.

Prudence moved to help him, letting her own hands run under his jacket to his shirt. He released her and suddenly sat up.

"What is it?" she whispered.

His reply was muffled by fabric as he stripped off his coat and pulled his shirt off over his head. The strong, lean shapes of his body danced with light and shadows as the firelight caressed them.

"We shall burn it away," he said fiercely. "Every last vestige of foolishness. But only if you will marry me, Prudence."

"It is too much to ask!" She sat up and put her hands on his shoulders. His skin was warm and smooth. "Why should you give up everything you have known? Forget marriage. I shall love you anyway."

She leaned forward and kissed his chest. A fast intake of breath made his muscles leap under her fingers. Prudence touched his small, hard nipple with her mouth and felt his response burn in answer to her own.

But he took her head in his hands and kissed her again on the lips. Then he gazed down at her, his eyes as dark as the midnight ocean. "Promise to marry me, or I shall walk out of your life. I will not make you my whore, Prudence. I want us to have children. I want us to be together when we're old and roaring with gout. I want the man at your hearth with the double-barreled shooting piece to be *me*. I want us *married*.''

"It's too great a sacrifice for you," said Prudence. "You are the son of an earl! I won't do it."

"Then I won't, in spite of a desire that is searing my very soul and tearing my mind into shreds, make love to you. I want you, Prudence, in the light of these flames, and your skin burning against mine." He took her hand and kissed it in the center of the palm. "I want to show you how to fly. But if you deny me your promise, it's over, now. Marry me!"

"Good heavens," said a cool voice from the doorway. "I really think you had better, after this."

Prudence looked up, over Harry's shoulder. Lady Acton stood smiling in the doorway with her hand on the knob.

"Pray, put on your shirt, Harry, and help Miss Drake to get decent."

"But I am—"

Harry looked at her and laughed, entirely without rancor or shame. He rolled back onto the hearth rug and gave way to a great shout of hilarity.

Prudence looked at his face, relaxed and open in genuine amusement. Dear God, how she loved him! Then she glanced down at herself and blushed scarlet. How had he done it? Her skirts were nearly around her waist, revealing a humiliating length of stocking above her sensible black boots. Her dress was unbuttoned. The ties of her shift lay open to reveal her naked breasts. They were swollen and aching, and her nipples were shamelessly puckered into hard nubs, like thimbles. She grabbed at her dress, but Harry's hands were there first. He gently pulled the fabric together and made deft little bows in the ties, then buttoned all the fastenings at the front of her dress, before kissing her once more, briefly, on the forehead.

"Tell her she must marry me, Mother," he said. "And I

will forgive myself enough to make you the apology I owe you.''

''But I cannot,'' wailed Prudence. ''You are ill and hurting! You don't think what you ask!''

''Yes, I do. My headache has gone away. It went away when you told me you loved me. *With all my heart,* you said. As I love you, Prudence Drake. So now we shall marry and live happily ever after.''

Prudence turned to Harry's mother. ''Lady Acton, you told me yourself that it would be impossible!''

''I have changed my mind, my dear. I would like you for a daughter very much. You have my blessing for a match. And as for the rest—Lord Belham has a plan.''

Epilogue

There was the sudden shriek of an eagle high overhead. Harry pulled up the curricle and took Prudence by the hand.

"Dear God, how green it has become since we were here with Richard and my mother! And the flowers, Prudence!

'There was a time when meadow, grove and stream,
The earth and every common sight,
To me did seem
Appareled in celestial light.'

But it's not in the past, it's now and the future. I had no idea that Scotland could be so blessed. Nor I, of course!" He carried her hand to his lips and kissed it, laughing. "I believe we are home, angel. That must be it!"

Prudence looked away down the stony track where he was pointing. Ahead of them lay a rich valley, with scattered groves of trees sheltering the meadows which ran down to the loch. Beneath the trees and over the rising skirts of the mountains the green was scintillating with wildflowers. Fluffy specks of catkin down danced and sparkled in the golden air. At the end of the valley stood a crenellated house, white stone walls gleaming under the cobalt sky. Clusters of round turrets sat at each corner, their conical roofs reaching up against the towering backdrop of Beinn Mhor.

"It's beautiful!" exclaimed Prudence.

The horse shifted a little and mouthed at the bit. Harry gently corrected it. "How sad that Bobby's father never lived in it."

Prudence smiled at him and laid her head on his shoulder. "It was built for love. Lord Belham says that his son, Henry, built it for his wife, but she died before they could move in. He took Bobby to London and refused to come back here. But it's part of Bobby's inheritance now."

"And our home until the young Lord Dunraven comes of age. You don't regret anything, do you, Prudence?"

She sat up and laughed at him. "To live here with you and Bobby? How could I? What more in life could I possibly want?"

"To have had a grand English wedding?"

"I'm perfectly content with my plain Scots one at Gretna Green. We are probably the only couple to have been married there twice. Though I wish, of course, that all your family could have been there, instead of only Richard. I am sorry for that."

"My father controls the others—and my mother didn't dare risk coming to Scotland again. But it doesn't matter. They will each visit when they come of age."

"Lord Acton did terrify me, Harry, calling for his solicitors to strike you from the will, stopping your allowance! Will he truly refuse ever to see you again?"

Harry shrugged. "We shan't need the money. But yes, I'm sorry too. He is my father, after all. He may come around eventually. Mother and Richard will work on him. Richard isn't so far away at Acton Mead. Though he and father never did get along, now Helena is carrying the next heir it's their turn to do no wrong, poor souls. I can't wait until she has the baby and they can visit us up here. And one day you will meet my sisters. Mother is planning to give my sister Eleanor her come out in London this month. Father will be there, of course, surrounded by all the eligible young ladies I *should* have married!" He laughed and stretched with exultant pleasure. "So it may take some time. But we have each other and we have forever."

"In the meantime you and I will work for Lord Belham running Bobby's estates and taking care of him . . ."

"And on new pistol designs for His Majesty's government . . ."

"—using old Lady Dunraven's workshops at Dunraven Keep!"

The eagle shrieked again. Harry looked up at it and Prudence followed his gaze. But she did not pay much attention to the powerful bird soaring golden in the sunshine, she was looking at the line of Harry's throat and thinking of how soon she would be able to get him inside and peel off that silly cravat and his waistcoat and his shirt . . .

"Mr. and Mrs. MacEwen will be here next week and I want to discuss some of my ideas with him. Dear God, the Manse seems a lifetime ago! How could I ever have been foolish enough to believe that Lord Belham meant Bobby harm?"

"Because I told you so, of course."

"Yet it seems, angel, that from the day I opened my eyes on that beach and saw your beautiful face looking down at me, everything I did was a lunatic failure."

Prudence laughed at him. "You didn't fail with me!"

"No, for you have married me and I have found my ramshackle self at last!"

"You were always there," said Prudence. "Underneath Mr. Grey and Hal and Mr. Herdriver and your father's favorite, and in spite of all the people who wanted to knock you over the head or drive you into becoming a nick ninny, you were always there and I will always love you."

He kissed her with a luxuriant slowness until Prudence pulled away and laughed again. "Oh, gracious! Come, husband,

Bobby will be here at any moment. See over there? That's the track over Beinn Mhor where Sergeant Keen is bringing him on his pony. I want the doors open for him, at least.''

"And I want your hair down and your—"

Prudence clapped her hand over his mouth. "Let us at least get to the house!"

Harry kissed her palm and glanced once again at Dunraven House, glimmering its welcome in the warm valley.

"After that grim medieval keep, angel, I really didn't expect this. To find such a house in Scotland, of all places!"

"It's the French influence," said Prudence. *"The Auld Alliance.* Many Scottish houses are built to look like chateaux on the Loire."

"Is that what it is?" Harry grinned down at her before beginning to kiss her again, his brilliant passion finding fervent echo in her response. "It looks like a fairy-tale castle to me."

Author's Note

This story was originally inspired by a child on a beach who said to me exactly what Bobby first says to Prudence—but it was in Ireland. To move the beach to Scotland and have Bobby enthralled by the myth of the silkie led to all the rest.

Serious canal building in Britain began when the Duke of Bridgewater cut his famous waterway to deliver coal to Manchester. It continued throughout the Regency, eventually resulting in over twelve thousand miles of canals. The Harecastle Tunnel on the Grand Trunk Canal which *The White Lady* must be "legged through" took six hundred "navigators" (whence: navvy, a laborer) eleven years of ceaseless toil. It remained in use into the twentieth century, although a second tunnel was built parallel to it in 1824. But, alas, canals were to be doomed by the introduction of the railway. As the Duke of Bridgewater said: "Well, they will last my time, but I see mischief in those damned tramroads." Today fewer than three thousand miles of these quiet waterways remain. I have taken some small liberties in my description of life on a "narrow boat'' (they are not called barges), but this is a romance, after all!

The pistol of the early nineteenth century was a hand made flintlock—ignition of priming provided by sparks from a flint striking steel, and the Regency brought the art of the gunsmith to its zenith. Yet the flintlock had its drawbacks: besides giving off black smoke when fired, there was a distinct delay between pulling the trigger and firing, and it would not fire at all if the powder was damp or if the priming failed to ignite the main charge—a ''flash in the pan''.

In 1807 a Scottish minister, Alexander Forsyth, patented the first detonating lock and the hunt was on for a replacement for the flintlock mechanism. The new principle involved a chemical compound which detonated when struck by a hammer, thus doing away with the capricious priming powder. Unhindered by a patent which applied only in Britain, French gunsmiths continued to experiment with detonating locks. Meanwhile many British (and American) gunsmiths were busy with inventions of their own. When Forsyth's patent ran out in 1821 the copper percussion cap showed the most promise of the many ideas tested. Within twenty years flintlocks were essentially obsolete and firearms had become infinitely more deadly—but how could Harry have foreseen the mayhem which would finally result?

Folly's Reward is the fifth in my Regency *Reward* series which began with the award-winning *Scandal's Reward* in 1994. Harry first appeared in *Virtue's Reward,* where you may discover more about his previous adventures with Richard and Helena. I owe many thanks to everyone who wrote and asked me to give Harry his own book. It took some surprising turns, didn't it? I do hope you'll agree it was worth the wait!

The Actons also star in *Rogue's Reward* (1995), the story of Richard and Harry's sister Eleanor and an entirely ineligible rake. Discerning readers will realize that although *Rogue's Reward* was published first, that story takes place later than *Folly's Reward.* But although they share characters the stories are quite independent, so I hope you'll forgive me. The final book in this series, *Love's Reward,* involves the Acton sister who is most like Harry: wild, dark-haired Joanna. Look for *Love's Reward* toward the end of 1997.

I love to hear from readers. If you'd like to write to P.O. Box 197, Ridgway, CO 81432 and enclose a long self-addressed stamped envelope, I'll be happy to send you complete details of all my *Rewards* of the Regency!

LOOK FOR THESE REGENCY ROMANCES

ROMANCE FROM JO BEVERLY

DANGEROUS JOY   (0-8217-5129-8, $5.99)

FORBIDDEN   (0-8217-4488-7, $4.99)

THE SHATTERED ROSE   (0-8217-5310-X, $5.99)

TEMPTING FORTUNE   (0-8217-4858-0, $4.99)

WATCH FOR THESE REGENCY ROMANCES